Family Happiness

Leo Tolstoy

PART I

CHAPTER 1

We were in mourning for my mother, who had died in the autumn, and I spent all that winter alone in the country with Katya and Sonya.

Katya was an old friend of the family, our governess who had brought us all up, and I had known and loved her since my earliest recollections. Sonya was my younger sister. It was a dark and sad winter which we spent in our old house of Pokrovskoye. The weather was cold and so windy that the snowdrifts came higher than the windows; the panes were almost always dimmed by frost, and we seldom walked or drove anywhere throughout the winter. Our visitors were few, and those who came brought no addition of cheerfulness or happiness to the household. They all wore sad faces and spoke low, as if they were afraid of waking someone; they never laughed, but sighed and often shed tears as they looked at me and especially at little Sonya in her black frock. The feeling of death clung to the house; the air was still filled with the grief and horror of death. My mother's room was kept locked; and whenever I passed it on my way to bed, I felt a strange uncomfortable impulse to look into that cold empty room.

I was then seventeen; and in the very year of her death my mother was intending to move to Petersburg, in order to take me into society. The loss of my mother was a great grief to me; but I must confess to another feeling behind that grief — a feeling that though I was young and pretty (so everybody told me), I was wasting a second winter in the solitude of the country. Before the winter ended, this sense of dejection, solitude, and simple boredom increased to such an extent that I refused to leave my room or open the piano or take up a book. When Katya urged me to find some occupation, I said that I did not feel able for it; but in my heart I said, "What is the good of it? What is the good of doing anything, when the best part of my life is being wasted like this?" and to this question, tears were my only answer.

I was told that I was growing thin and losing my looks; but even this failed to interest me. What did it matter? For whom? I felt that my whole life was bound to go on in the same solitude and helpless dreariness, from which I had myself no strength and even no wish to escape. Towards the end of winter Katya became anxious about me and determined to make an effort to take me abroad. But money was needed for this, and we hardly knew how our affairs stood after my mother's death. Our guardian, who was to come and clear up our position, was expected every day.

In March he arrived.

"Well, thank God!" Katya said to me one day, when I was walking up and down the room like a shadow, without occupation, without a thought, and without a wish. "Sergey Mikhaylych has arrived; he has sent to inquire about us and means to come here for dinner. You must rouse yourself, dear Mashechka," she added, "or what will he think of you? He was so fond of you all."

Sergey Mikhaylych was our near neighbor, and, though a much younger man, had been a friend of my father's. His coming was likely to change our plans and to make it possible to leave the country; and also I had grown up in the habit of love and regard for him; and when Katya begged me to rouse myself, she guessed rightly that it would give me especial pain to show to disadvantage before him, more than before any other of our friends. Like everyone in the house, from Katya and his god-daughter Sonya down to the helper in the stables, I loved him from old habit; and also he had a special significance for me, owing to a remark which my mother had once made in my presence. "I should like you to marry a man like him," she said. At the time this seemed to me strange and even unpleasant. My ideal husband was quite different: he was to be thin, pale, and sad; and Sergey Mikhaylych was middle-aged, tall, robust, and always, as it seemed to me, in good spirits. But still my mother's words stuck in my head; and even six years before this time, when I was eleven, and he still said "thou" to me, and played with me, and called me by the pet-name of "violet" — even then I sometimes asked myself in a fright, "What shall I do, if he suddenly wants to marry me?"

Before our dinner, to which Katya made an addition of sweets and a dish of spinach, Sergey Mikhaylych arrived. From the window I watched him drive up to the house in a small sleigh; but as soon as it turned the corner, I hastened to the drawing room, meaning to pretend that his visit was a complete surprise. But when I heard his tramp and loud voice and Katya's footsteps in the hall, I lost patience and went to meet him myself. He was holding Katya's hand, talking loud, and smiling. When he saw me, he stopped and looked at me for a time without bowing. I was uncomfortable and felt myself blushing.

"Can this be really you?" he said in his plain decisive way, walking towards me with his arms apart. "Is so great a change possible? How grown-up you are! I used to call you "violet", but now you are a rose in full bloom!'

He took my hand in his own large hand and pressed it so hard that it almost hurt. Expecting him to kiss my hand, I bent towards him, but he only pressed it again and looked straight into my eyes with the old firmness and cheerfulness in his face.

It was six years since I had seen him last. He was much changed — older and darker in complexion; and he now wore whiskers which did not become him at all; but much remained the same — his simple manner, the large features of his honest open face, his bright intelligent eyes, his friendly, almost boyish, smile.

Five minutes later he had ceased to be a visitor and had become the friend of us all, even of the servants, whose visible eagerness to wait on him proved their pleasure at his arrival. He behaved quite unlike the neighbors who had visited us after my mother's death. they had thought it necessary to be silent when they sat with us, and to shed tears. He, on the contrary, was cheerful and talkative, and said not a word about my mother, so that this indifference seemed strange to me at first and even improper on the part of so close a friend. But I understood later that what seemed indifference was sincerity, and I felt grateful for it. In the evening Katya poured out tea, sitting in her old place in the drawing room, where she used to sit in my mother's lifetime; our old butler Grigori had hunted out one of my father's pipes and brought it to him; and he began to walk up and down the room as he used to do in past days.

"How many terrible changes there are in this house, when one thinks of it all!" he said, stopping in his walk.

"Yes," said Katya with a sigh; and then she put the lid on the samovar and looked at him, quite ready to burst out crying.

"I suppose you remember your father?" he said, turning to me.

"Not clearly," I answered.

"How happy you would have been together now!" he added in a low voice, looking thoughtfully at my face above the eyes. "I was very fond of him," he added in a still lower tone, and it seemed to me that his eyes were shining more than usual.

"And now God has taken her too!" said Katya; and at once she laid her napkin on the teapot, took out her handkerchief, and began to cry.

"Yes, the changes in this house are terrible," he repeated, turning away. "Sonya, show me your toys," he added after a little and went off to the parlor. When he had gone, I looked at Katya with eyes full of tears.

"What a splendid friend he is!" she said. And, though he was no relation, I did really feel a kind of warmth and comfort in the sympathy of this good man.

I could hear him moving about in the parlor with Sonya, and the sound of her high childish voice. I sent tea to him there; and I heard him sit down at the piano and strike the keys with Sonya's little hands.

Then his voice came — "Marya Aleksandrovna, come here and play something."

I liked his easy behavior to me and his friendly tone of command; I got up and went to him.

"Play this," he said, opening a book of Beethoven's music at the adagio of the "Moonlight Sonata." "Let me hear how you play," he added, and went off to a corner of the room, carrying his cup with him.

I somehow felt that with him it was impossible to refuse or to say beforehand that I played badly: I sat down obediently at the piano and began to play as well as I could; yet I was afraid of criticism, because I knew that he understood and enjoyed music. The adagio suited the remembrance of past days evoked by our conversation at tea, and I believe that I played it fairly well. But he would not let me play the scherzo. "No," he said, coming up to me; "you don't play that right; don't go on; but the first movement was not bad; you seem to be musical." This moderate praise pleased me so much that I even reddened. I felt it pleasant and strange that a friend of my father's, and his contemporary, should no longer treat me like a child but speak to me seriously. Katya now went upstairs to put Sonya to bed, and we were left alone in the parlor.

He talked to me about my father, and about the beginning of their friendship and the happy days they had spent together, while I was still busy with lesson-books and toys; and his talk put my father before me in quite a new light, as a man of simple and delightful character. He asked me too about my tastes, what I read and what I intended to do, and gave me advice. The man of mirth and jest who used to tease me and make me toys had disappeared; here was a serious, simple, and affectionate friend, for whom I could not help feeling respect and sympathy. It was easy and pleasant to talk to him; and yet I felt an involuntary strain also. I was anxious about each word I spoke: I wished so much to earn for my own sake the love which had been given me already merely because I was my father's daughter.

After putting Sonya to bed, Katya joined us and began to complain to him of my apathy, about which I had said nothing.

"So she never told me the most important thing of all!" he said, smiling and shaking his head reproachfully at me.

"Why tell you?" I said. "It is very tiresome to talk about, and it will pass off." (I really felt now, not only that my dejection would pass off, but that it had already passed off, or rather had never existed.)

"It is a bad thing," he said, "not to be able to stand solitude. Can it be that you are a young lady?"

"Of course, I am a young lady," I answered laughing.

"Well, I can't praise a young lady who is alive only when people are admiring her, but as soon as she is left alone, collapses and finds nothing to her taste — one who is all for show and has no resources in herself."

"You have a flattering opinion of me!" I said, just for the sake of saying something.

He was silent for a little. Then he said: "Yes; your likeness to your father means something. There is something in you . . .," and his kind attentive look again flattered me and made me feel a pleasant embarrassment.

I noticed now for the first time that his face, which gave one at first the impression of high spirits, had also an expression peculiar to himself — bright at first and then more and more attentive and rather sad.

"You ought not to be bored and you cannot be," he said; "you have music, which you appreciate, books, study; your whole life lies before you, and now or never is the time to prepare for it and save yourself future regrets. A year hence it will be too late."

He spoke to me like a father or an uncle, and I felt that he kept a constant check upon himself, in order to keep on my level. Though I was hurt that he considered me as inferior to himself, I was pleased that for me alone he thought it necessary to try to be different.

For the rest of the evening he talked about business with Katya.

"Well, goodby, dear friends," he said. Then he got up, came towards me and took my hand. When shall we see you again?" asked Katya.

"In spring," he answered, still holding my hand. "I shall go now to Danilovka" (this was another property of ours), "look into things there and make what arrangements I can; then I go to Moscow on business of my own; and in summer we shall meet again."

"Must you really be away so long?" I asked, and I felt terribly grieved. I had really hoped to see him every day, and I felt a sudden shock of regret, and a fear that my depression would return. And my face and voice just have made this plain.

"You must find more to do and not get depressed," he said; and I thought his tone too cool and unconcerned. "I shall put you through an examination in spring," he added, letting go my hand and not looking at me.

When we saw him off in the hall, he put on his fur coat in a hurry and still avoided looking at me. "He is taking a deal of trouble for nothing!" I thought. "Does he think me so anxious that he should look at me? He is a good man, a very good man; but that's all."

That evening, however, Katya and I sat up late, talking, not about him but about our plans for the summer, and where we should spend next winter and what we should do then. I had ceased to ask that terrible question — what is the good of it all? Now it seemed quite plain and simple: the proper object of life was happiness, and I promised myself much happiness ahead. It seemed as if our gloomy old house had suddenly become fully of light and life.

CHAPTER 2

Meanwhile spring arrived. My old dejection passed away and gave place to the unrest which spring brings with it, full of dreams and vague hopes and desires. Instead of living as I had done at the beginning of winter, I read and played the piano and gave lessons to Sonya; but also I often went into the garden and wandered for long alone through the avenues, or sat on a bench there; and Heaven knows what my thoughts and wishes and hopes were at such times. Sometimes at night, especially if there was a moon, I sat by my bedroom window till dawn; sometimes, when Katya was not watching, I stole out into the garden wearing only a wrapper and ran through the dew as far as the pond; and once I went all the way to the open fields and walked right round the garden alone at night.

I find it difficult now to recall and understand the dreams which then filled my imagination. Even when I can recall them, I find it hard to believe that my dreams were just like that: they were so strange and so remote from life. Sergey Mikhaylych kept his promise: he returned from his travels at the end of May. His first visit to us was in the evening and was quite unexpected. We were sitting in the veranda, preparing for tea. By this time the garden was all green, and the nightingales had taken up their quarters for the whole of St. Peter's Fast in the leafy borders. The tops of the round lilac bushes had a sprinkling of white and purple — a sign that their flowers were ready to open. The foliage of the birch avenue was all transparent in the light of the setting sun. In the veranda there was shade and freshness. The evening dew was sure to be heavy in the grass. Out of doors beyond the garden the last sounds of day were audible, and the noise of the sheep and cattle, as they were driven home. Nikon, the half-witted boy, was driving his water-cart along the path outside the veranda, and a cold stream of water from the sprinkler made dark circles on the mould round the stems and supports of the dahlias. In our veranda the polished samovar shone and hissed on the white table-cloth; there were cracknels and biscuits and cream on the table. Katya was busy washing the cups with her plump hands. I was too hungry after bathing to wait for tea, and was eating bread with thick fresh cream. I was wearing a gingham blouse with loose sleeves, and my hair, still wet, was covered with a kerchief. Katya saw him first, even before he came in.

"You, Sergey Mikhaylych!" she cried. "Why, we were just talking about you."

I got up, meaning to go and change my dress, but he caught me just by the door.

"Why stand on such ceremony in the country?" he said, looking with a smile at the kerchief on my head. "You don't mind the presence of your butler, and I am really the same to you as Grigori is." But I felt just then that he was looking at me in a way quite unlike Grigori's way, and I was uncomfortable.

"I shall come back at once," I said, as I left them.

"But what is wrong?" he called out after me; "it's just the dress of a young peasant woman."

"How strangely he looked at me!" I said to myself as I was quickly changing upstairs. "Well, I'm glad he has come; things will be more lively." After a look in the glass I ran gaily downstairs and into the veranda; I was out of breath and did not disguise my haste. He was sitting at the table, talking to Katya about our affairs. He glanced at me and smiled; then he went on talking. From what he said it appeared that our affairs were in capital shape: it was now possible for us, after spending the summer in the country, to go either to Petersburg for Sonya's education, or abroad.

"If only you would go abroad with us —" said Katya; "without you we shall be quite lost there."

"Oh, I should like to go round the world with you," he said, half in jest and half in earnest.

"All right," I said; let us start off and go round the world."

He smiled and shook his head.

"What about my mother? What about my business, he said. "But that's not the question just now: I want to know how you have been spending your time. Not depressed again, I hope?

When I told him that I had been busy and not bored during his absence, and when Katya confirmed my report, he praised me as if he had a right to do so, and his words and looks were kind, as they might have been to a child. I felt obliged to tell him, in detail and with perfect frankness, all my good actions, and to confess, as if I were in church, all that he might disapprove of.

The evening was so fine that we stayed in the veranda after tea was cleared away; and the conversation interested me so much that I did not notice how we ceased by degrees to hear any sound of the servants indoors. The scent of flowers grew stronger and came from all sides; the grass was drenched with dew; a nightingale struck up in a lilac bush close by and then stopped on hearing our voices; the starry sky seemed to come down lower over our heads.

It was growing dusk, but I did not notice it till a bat suddenly and silently flew in beneath the veranda awning and began to flutter round my white shawl. I shrank back against the wall and nearly cried out; but the bat as silently and swiftly dived out from under the awning and disappeared in the half-darkness of the garden.

"How fond I am of this place of yours!" he said, changing the conversation; "I wish I could spend all my life here, sitting in this veranda."

"Well, do then!" said Katya.

"That's all very well," he said, "but life won't sit still."

"Why don't you marry?" asked Katya; you would make an excellent husband.

"Because I like sitting still?" and he laughed. "No, Katerina Karlovna, too late for you and me to marry. People have long ceased to think of me as a marrying man, and I am even surer of it myself; and I declare I have felt quite comfortable since the matter was settled."

It seemed to me that he said this in an unnaturally persuasive way.

"Nonsense!" said Katya; "a man of thirty-six makes out that he is too old!"

"Too old indeed," he went on, "when all one wants is to sit still. For a man who is going to marry that's not enough. Just you ask her," he added, nodding at me; "people of her age should marry, and you and I can rejoice in their happiness."

The sadness and constraint latent in his voice was not lost upon me. He was silent for a little, and neither Katya nor I spoke.

"Well, just fancy," he went on, turning a little on his seat; "suppose that by some mischance I married a girl of seventeen, Masha, if you like — I mean, Marya Aleksandrovna. The instance is good; I am glad it turned up; there could not be a better instance."

I laughed; but I could not understand why he was glad, or what it was that had turned up.

"Just tell me honestly, with your hand on your heart," he said, turning as if playfully to me, "would it not be a misfortune for you to unite your life with that of an old worn-out man who only wants to sit still, whereas Heaven knows what wishes are fermenting in that heart of yours?"

I felt uncomfortable and was silent, not knowing how to answer him.

"I am not making you a proposal, you know," he said, laughing; "but am I really the kind of husband you dream of when walking alone in the avenue at twilight? It would be a misfortune, would it not?"

"No, not a misfortune," I began.

"But a bad thing," he ended my sentence.

"Perhaps; but I may be mistaken . . ." He interrupted me again.

"There, you see! She is quite right, and I am grateful to her for her frankness, and very glad to have had this conversation. And there is something else to be said" — he added: "for me too it would be a very great misfortune."

"How odd you are! You have not changed in the least," said Katya, and then left the veranda, to order supper to be served.

When she had gone, we were both silent and all was still around us, but for one exception. A nightingale, which had sung last night by fitful snatches, now flooded the garden with a steady stream of song, and was soon answered by another from the dell below, which had not sung till that evening. The nearer bird stopped and seemed to listen for a moment, and then broke out again still louder than before, pouring out his song in piercing long drawn cadences. There was a regal calm in the birds' voices, as they floated through the realm of night which belongs to those birds and not to man. The gardener walked past to his sleeping-quarters in the greenhouse, and the noise of his heavy boots grew fainter and fainter along the path. Someone whistled twice sharply at the foot of the hill; and then all was still again. The rustling of leaves could just be heard; the veranda awning flapped; a faint perfume, floating in the air, came down on the veranda and filled it. I felt silence awkward after what had been said, but what to say I did not know. I looked at him. His eyes, bright in the half-darkness, turned towards me.

"How good life is!" he said.

I sighed, I don't know why.

"Well?" he asked.

"Life is good," I repeated after him.

Again we were silent, and again I felt uncomfortable. I could not help fancying that I had wounded him by agreeing that he was old; and I wished to comfort him but did not know how.

"Well, I must be saying good-bye," he said, rising; "my mother expects me for supper; I have hardly seen her all day."

"I meant to play you the new sonata," I said.

"That must wait," he replied; and I thought that he spoke coldly.

"Good-bye."

I felt still more certain that I had wounded him, and I was sorry. Katya and I went to the steps to see him off and stood for a while in the open, looking along the road where he had disappeared from view. When we ceased to hear the sound of his horse's hoofs, I walked round the house to the veranda, and again sat looking into the garden; and all I wished to see and hear, I still saw and heard for a long time in the dewy mist filled with the sounds of night.

He came a second time, and a third; and the awkwardness arising from that strange conversation passed away entirely, never to return. During that whole summer he came two or three times a week; and I grew so accustomed to his presence, that, when he failed to come for some time, Ii missed him and felt angry with him, and thought he was behaving badly in deserting me. He treated me like a boy whose company he liked, asked me questions, invited the most cordial frankness on my part, gave me advice and encouragement, or sometimes scolded and checked me. But in spite of his constant effort to keep on my level, I was aware that behind the part of him which I could understand there remained an entire region of mystery, into which he did not consider it necessary to admit me; and this fact did much to preserve my respect for him and his attraction for me. I knew from Katya and from our neighbors that he had not only to care for his old mother with whom he lived, and to manage his own estate and our affairs, but was also responsible for some public business which was the source of serious worries; but what view he took of all this, what were his convictions, plans, and hopes, I could not in the least find out from him. Whenever I turned the conversation to his affairs, he frowned in a way peculiar to himself and seemed to imply, "Please stop! That is no business of yours;" and then he changed the subject. This hurt me at first; but I soon grew accustomed to confining our talk to my affairs, and felt this to be quite natural.

There was another thing which displeased me at first and then became pleasant to me. This was his complete indifference and even contempt for my personal appearance. Never by word or look did he imply that I was pretty; on the contrary, he frowned and laughed, whenever the word was applied to me in his presence. He even liked to find fault with my looks and tease me about them. On special days Katya liked to dress me out in fine clothes and to arrange my hair effectively; but my finery met only with mockery from him, which pained kind-hearted Katya and at first disconcerted me. She had made up her mind that he admired me; and she could not understand how a man could help wishing a woman whom he admired to appear to the utmost advantage. But I soon understood what he wanted. He wished to make sure that I had not a trace of affectation. And when I understood this I was really quite free from affectation in the clothes I wore, or the arrangement of my hair, or my movements; but a very obvious form of affectation took its place — an affectation of simplicity, at a time when I could not yet be really simple. That he loved me, I knew; but I did not yet ask myself whether he loved me as a child or as a woman. I valued his love; I felt that he thought me better than all other young women in the world, and I could not help wishing him to go on being deceived about me. Without wishing to deceive him, I did deceive him, and I became better myself while deceiving him. I felt it a better and worthier course to show him to good points of my heart and mind than of my body. My hair, hands, face, ways — all these, whether good or bad, he had appraised at once and knew so well, that I could add nothing to my external appearance except the wish to deceive him. But my mind and heart he did not know, because he loved them, and because they were in the very process of growth and development; and on this point I could and did deceive him. And how easy I felt in his company, once I understood this clearly! My causeless bashfulness and awkward movements completely disappeared. Whether he saw me from in front, or in profile, sitting or standing, with my hair up or my hair down, I felt that he knew me from head to foot, and I fancied, was satisfied with me as I was. If, contrary to his habit, he had suddenly said to me as other people did, that I had a pretty face, I believe that I should not have liked it at all. But, on the other hand, how light and happy my heart was when, after I had said something, he looked hard at me and said, hiding emotion under a mask of raillery:

"Yes, there is something in you! you are a fine girl — that I must tell you."

And for what did I receive such rewards, which filled my heart with pride and joy? Merely for saying that I felt for old Grigori in his love for his little granddaughter; or because the reading of some poem or novel moved me to tears; or because I liked Mozart better than Schulhof. And I was surprised at my own quickness in guessing what was good and worthy of love, when I certainly did not know then what was good and worthy to be loved. Most of my former tastes and habits did not please him; and a mere look of his, or a twitch of his eyebrow was enough to show that he did not like what I was trying to say; and I felt at once that my own standard was changed. Sometimes, when he was about to give me a piece of advice, I seemed to know before hand what he would say. When he looked in my face and asked me a question, his very look would draw out of me the answer he wanted. All my thoughts and feelings of that time were not really mine: they were his thoughts and feelings, which had suddenly become mine and passed into my life and lighted it up. Quite unconsciously I began to look at everything with different eyes — at Katya and the servants and Sonya and myself and my occupations. Books, which I used to read merely to escape boredom, now became one of the chief pleasures of my life, merely because he brought me the books and we read and discussed them together. The lessons I gave to Sonya had been a burdensome obligation which I forced myself to go through from a sense of duty; but, after he was present at a lesson, it became a joy to me to watch Sonya's progress. It used to seem to me an impossibility to learn a whole piece of music by heart; but now, when I knew that he would hear it and might praise it, I would play a single movement forty times over without stopping, till poor Katya stuffed her ears with cottonwool, while I was still not weary of it. The same old sonatas seemed quite different in the expression, and came out quite changed and much improved. Even Katya, whom I knew and loved like a second self, became different in my eyes. I now understood for the first time that she was not in the least bound to be the mother, friend, and slave that she was to us. Now I appreciated all the self-sacrifice and devotion of this affectionate creature, and all my obligations to her; and I began to love her even better. It was he too who taught me to take quite a new view of our serfs and servants and maids. It is an absurd confession to make — but I had spent seventeen years among these people and yet knew less about than about strangers whom I had never seen; it had never once occurred to me that they had their affections and wishes and sorrows, just as I had. Our garden and woods and fields which I had known so long, became suddenly new and beautiful to me. He was right in saying that the only certain happiness in life is to live for others. At the time his words seemed to me strange, and I did not understand them; but by degrees this became a conviction with me, without thinking about it. He revealed to me a whole new world of joys in the present, without changing anything in my life, without adding anything except himself to each impression in my mind. All that had surrounded me from childhood without saying anything to me, suddenly came to life. The mere sight of him made everything begin to speak and press for admittance to my heart, filling it with happiness.

Often during that summer, when I went upstairs to my room and lay down on my bed, the old unhappiness of spring with its desires and hopes for the future gave place to a passionate happiness in the present. Unable to sleep, I often got up and sat on Katya's bed and told her how perfectly happy I was, though I now realize that this was quite unnecessary, as she could see it for herself.

But when told me that she was quite content and perfectly happy, and kissed me. I believed her — it seemed to me so necessary and just that everyone should be happy. But Katya could think of sleep too; and sometimes, pretending to be angry, she drove me from her bed and went to sleep, while I turned over and over in my mind all that made me so happy. Sometimes I got up and said my prayers over again, praying in my own words and thanking God for all the happiness he had given me.

All was quiet in the room; there was only the even breathing of Katya in her sleep, and the ticking of the clock by her bed, while I turned from side to side and whispered words of prayer, or crossed myself and kissed the cross round my neck. The door was shut and the windows shuttered; perhaps a fly or gnat hung buzzing in the air. I felt a wish never to leave that room — a wish that dawn might never come, that my present frame of mind might never change. I felt that my dreams and thoughts and prayers were live things, living there in the dark with me, hovering about my bed, and standing over me. And every thought was his thought, and every feeling his feeling. I did not know yet that this was love; I though that things might go on so for ever, and that this feeling involved no consequences.

CHAPTER 3

One day when the corn was being carried, I went with Katya and Sonya to our favorite seat in the garden, in the shade of the lime trees and above the dell, beyond which the fields and woods lay open before us. It was three days since Sergey Mikhaylych had been to see us; we were expecting him, all the more because our bailiff reported that he had promised to visit the harvest field. At two o'clock we saw him ride on to the rye field. with a smile and a glance at me, Katya ordered peaches and cherries, of which he was very fond, to be brought; then she lay down on the bench and began to doze. I tore off a crooked flat lime tree branch, which made my hand wet with its juicy leaves and juicy bark. then I fanned Katya with it and went on with my book, breaking off from time to time, to look at the field path along which he must come. Sonya was making a dolls' house at the root of an old lime tree. The day was sultry, windless, and steaming; the clouds were packing and growing blacker; all morning a thunderstorm had been gathering, and I felt restless, as I always did before thunder. But by afternoon the clouds began to part, the sun sailed out into a clear sky, and only in one quarter was there a faint fumbling. A single heavy cloud, lowering above the horizon and mingling with the dust from the fields, was rent from time to time by pale zigzags of lightning which ran down to the ground. It was clear that for today the storm would pass off, with us at all events. The road beyond the garden was visible in places, and we could see a procession of high creaking carts slowly moving along it with their load of sheaves, while the empty carts rattled at a faster pace to meet them, with swaying legs and shirts fluttering in them. The thick dust neither blew away nor settled down — it stood still beyond the fence, and we could see it through the transparent foliage of the garden trees. A little farther off, in the stackyard, the same voices and the same creaking of wheels were audible; and the same yellow sheaves that had moves slowly past the fence were now flying aloft, and I could see the oval stacks gradually rising higher, and their conspicuous pointed tops, and the laborers swarming upon them. On the dusty field in front more carts were moving and more yellow sheaves were visible; and the noise of the carts, with the sound of talking and singing, came to us from a distance. At one side the bare stubble, with strips of fallow covered with wormwood, came more and more into view. Lower down, to the right, the gay dresses of the women were visible, as they bent down and swung their arms to bind the sheaves. Here the bare stubble looked untidy; but the disorder was cleared by degrees, as the pretty sheaves were ranged at close intervals. It seemed as if summer had suddenly turned to autumn before my eyes. The dust and heat were everywhere, except in our favorite nook in the garden; and everywhere, in this heat and dust and under the burning sun, the laborers carried on their heavy task with talk and noise.

Meanwhile Katya slept so sweetly on our shady bench, beneath her white cambric handkerchief, the black juicy cherries glistened so temptingly on the plate, our dresses were so clean and fresh, the water in the jug was so bright with rainbow colors in the sun, and I felt so happy. "How can I help it?" I thought; "am I to blame for being happy? And how can I share my happiness? How and to whom can I surrender all myself and all my happiness?"

By this time the sun had sunk behind the tops of the birch avenue, the dust was settling on the fields, the distance became clearer and brighter in the slanting light. The clouds had dispersed altogether; I could see through the trees the thatch of three new corn stacks. The laborers came down off the stacks; the carts hurried past, evidently for the last time, with a loud noise of shouting; the women, with rakes over their shoulders and straw bands in their belts, walked home past us, singing loudly; and still there was no sign of Sergey Mikhaylych, though I had seen him ride down the hill long ago. Suddenly he appeared upon the avenue, coming from a quarter where I was not looking for him. He had walked round by the dell. He came quickly towards me, with his hat off and radiant with high spirits. Seeing that Katya was asleep, he bit his lip, closed his eyes, and advanced on tiptoe; I saw at once that he was in that peculiar mood of causeless merriment which I always delighted to see in him, and which we called "wild ecstasy". He was just like a schoolboy playing truant; his whole figure, from head to foot, breathed content, happiness, and boyish frolic.

"Well, young violet, how are you? All right?" he said in a whisper, coming up to me and taking my hand. Then, in answer to my question, "Oh, I'm splendid today, I feel like a boy of thirteen — I want to play at horses and climb trees."

"Is it wild ecstasy?" I asked, looking into his laughing eyes, and feeling that the "wild ecstasy" was infecting me.

"Yes," he answered, winking and checking a smile. "But I don't see why you need hit Katerina Karlovna on the nose."

With my eyes on him I had gone on waving the branch, without noticing that I had knocked the handkerchief off Katya's face and was now brushing her with the leaves. I laughed.

"She will say she was awake all the time," I whispered, as if not to awake Katya; but that was not my real reason — it was only that I liked to whisper to him.

He moved his lips in imitation of me, pretending that my voice was too low for him to hear. Catching sight of the dish of cherries, he pretended to steal it, and carried it off to Sonya under the lime tree, where he sat down on her dolls. Sonya was angry at first, but he soon made his peace with her by starting a game, to see which of them could eat cherries faster.

"If you like, I will send for more cherries," I said; "or let us go ourselves."

He took the dish and set the dolls on it, and we all three started for the orchard. Sonya ran behind us, laughing and pulling at his coat, to make him surrender the dolls. He gave them up and then turned to me, speaking more seriously.

"You really are a violet," he said, still speaking low, though there was no longer any fear of waking anybody; "when I came to you out of all that dust and heat and toil, I positively smelt violets at once. But not the sweet violet — you know, that early dark violet that smells of melting snow and spring grass."

"Is harvest going on well?" I asked, in order to hide the happy agitation which his words produced in me.

"First rate! Our people are always splendid. The more you know them, the better you like them."

"Yes," I said; "before you came I was watching them from the garden, and suddenly I felt ashamed to be so comfortable myself while they were hard at work, and so . . ."

He interrupted me, with a kind but grave look: "Don't talk like that, my dear; it is too sacred a matter to talk of lightly. God forbid that you should use fine phrases about that!"

"But it is only to you I say this."

"All right, I understand. But what about those cherries?"

The orchard was locked, and no gardener to be seen: he had sent them all off to help with the harvest. Sonya ran to fetch the key. But he would not wait for her: climbing up a corner of the wall, he raised the net and jumped down on the other side.

His voice came over the wall — "If you want some, give me the dish."

"No," I said; "I want to pick for myself. I shall fetch the key; Sonya won't find it."

But suddenly I felt that I must see what he was doing there and what he looked like — that I must watch his movements while he supposed that no one saw him. Besides I was simply unwilling just then to lose sight of him for a single minute. running on tiptoe through the nettles to the other side of the orchard where the wall was lower, I mounted on an empty cask, till the top of the wall was on a level with my waist, and then leaned over into the orchard. I looked at the gnarled old trees, with their broad dented leaves and the ripe black cherries hanging straight and heavy among the foliage; then I pushed my head under the net, and from under the knotted bough of an old cherry tree I caught sight of Sergey Mikhaylych. He evidently thought that I had gone away and that no one was watching him. With his hat off and his eyes shut, he was sitting on the fork of an old tree and carefully rolling into a ball a lump of cherry tree gum. Suddenly he shrugged his shoulders, opened his eyes, muttered something, and smiled. Both words and smile were so unlike him that I felt ashamed of myself for eavesdropping. It seemed to me that he had said, "Masha!" "Impossible," i thought. "Darling Masha!" he said again, in a lower and more tender tone. There was possible doubt about the two words this time. My heart beat hard, and such a passionate joy — illicit joy, as I felt — took hold of me, that I clutched at the wall, fearing to fall and betray myself. Startled by the sound of my movement, he looked round — he dropped his eyes instantly, and his face turned red, even scarlet, like a child's. He tried to speak, but in vain; again and again his face positively flamed up. Still he smiled as he looked at me, and I smiled too. Then his whole face grew radiant with happiness. He had ceased to be the old uncle who spoiled or scolded me; he was a man on my level, who loved and feared me as I loved and feared him. We looked at one another without speaking. But suddenly he frowned; the smile and light in his eyes disappeared, and he resumed his cold paternal tone, just as if we were doing something wrong and he was repenting and calling on me to repent.

"You had better get down, or you will hurt yourself," he said; "and do put your hair straight; just think what you look like?"

"What makes him pretend? what makes him want to give me pain?" I thought in my vexation. And the same instant brought an irresistible desire to upset his composure again and test my power over him.

"No," I said; "I mean to pick for myself." I caught hold of the nearest branch and climbed to the top of the wall; then, before he had time to catch me, I jumped down on the other side.

"What foolish things you do!" he muttered, flushing again and trying to hide his confusion under a pretence of annoyance; "you might really have hurt yourself. But how do you mean to get out of this?"

He was even more confused than before, but this time his confusion frightened rather than pleased me. It infected me too and made me blush; avoiding his eye and not knowing what to say, I began to pick cherries though I had nothing to put them in. I reproached myself, I repented of what I had done, I was frightened; I felt that I had lost his good opinion for ever by my folly. Both of us were silent and embarrassed. From this difficult situation Sonya rescued us by running back with the key in her hand. For some time we both addressed our conversation to her and said nothing to each other. When we returned to Katya, who assured us that she had never been asleep and was listening all the time, I calmed down, and he tried to drop into his fatherly patronizing manner again, but I was not taken in by it. A discussion which we had had some days before came back clear before me.

Katya had been saying that it was easier for a man to be in love and declare his love than for a woman.

"A man may say that he is in love, and a woman can't," she said.

"I disagree," said he; "a man has no business to say, and can't say that he is in love."

"Why not?" I asked.

"Because it never can be true. What sort of a revelation is that, that a man is in love? A man seems to think that whenever he says the word, something will go pop! — that some miracle will be worked, signs and wonders, with all the big guns firing at once! In my opinion," he went on, "whoever solemnly brings out the words "I love you" is either deceiving himself or, which is even worse, deceiving others."

"Then how is a woman to know that a man is in love with her, unless he tells her?" asked Katya.

"That I don't know," he answered; "every man has his own way of telling things. If the feeling exists, it will out somehow. But when I read novels, I always fancy the crestfallen look of Lieut. Strelsky or Alfred, when he says, "I love you, Eleanora", and expects something wonderful to happen at once, and no change at all takes place in either of them — their eyes and their noses and their whole selves remain exactly as they were."

Even then I had felt that this banter covered something serious that had reference to myself. But Katya resented his disrespectful treatment of the heroes in novels.

"You are never serious," she said; "but tell me truthfully, have you never yourself told a woman that you loved her?"

"Never, and never gone down on one knee," he answered, laughing; "and never will."

This conversation I now recalled, and i reflected that there was no need for him to tell me that he loved me. "I know that he loves me," I thought, "and all his endeavors to seem indifferent will not change my opinion."

He said little to me throughout the evening, but in every word he said to Katya and Sonya and in every look and movement of his I saw love and felt no doubt of it. I was only vexed and sorry for him, that he thought it necessary still to hide his feelings and pretend coldness, when it was all so clear, and when it would have been so simple and easy to be boundlessly happy. But my jumping down to him in the orchard weighed on me like a crime. I kept feeling that he would cease to respect me and was angry with me.

After tea I went to the piano, and he followed me.

"Play me something — it is long since I heard you," he said, catching me up in the parlor.

"I was just going to," I said. Then I looked straight in his face and said quickly, "Sergey Mikhaylych, you are not angry with me, are you?"

"What for?" he asked.

"For not obeying you this afternoon," I said, blushing.

He understood me: he shook his head and made a grimace, which implied that I deserved a scolding but that he did not feel able to give it.

"So it's all right, and we are friends again?" I said, sitting down at the piano.

"Of course!" he said.

In the drawing room, a large lofty room, there were only two lighted candles on the piano, the rest of the room remaining in half-darkness. Outside the open windows the summer night was bright. All was silent, except when the sound of Katya's footsteps in the unlighted parlor was heard occasionally, or when his horse, which was tied up under the window, snorted or stamped his hoof on the burdocks that grew there. He sat behind me, where I could not see him; but everywhere — in the half-darkness of the room, in every sound, in myself — I felt his presence. Every look, every movement of his, though I could not see them, found an echo in my heart. I played a sonata of Mozart's which he had brought me and which I had learnt in his presence and for him. I was not thinking at all of what I was playing, but I believe that I played it well, and I thought that he was pleased. I was conscious of his pleasure, and conscious too, though I never looked at him, of the gaze fixed on me from behind. Still moving my fingers mechanically. I turned round quite involuntarily and looked at him. The night had grown brighter, and his head stood out on a background of darkness. He was sitting with his head propped on his hands, and his eyes shone as they gazed at me. Catching his look, I smiled and stopped playing. He smiled too and shook his head reproachfully at the music, for me to go on. When I stopped, the moon had grown brighter and was riding high in the heavens; and the faint light of the candles was supplemented by a new silvery light which came in through the windows and fell on the floor. Katya called out that it was really too bad — that I had stopped at the best part of the piece, and that I was playing badly. But he declared that I had never played so well; and then he began to walk about the rooms — through the drawing room to the unlighted parlor and back again to the drawing room, and each time he looked at me and smiled. I smiled too; I wanted even to laugh with no reason; I was so happy at something that had happened that very day. Katya and I were standing by the piano; and each time that he vanished through the drawing room door, I started kissing her in my favorite place, the soft part of her neck under the chin; and each time he came back, I made a solemn face and refrained with difficulty from laughing.

"What is the matter with her today?" Katya asked him.

He only smiled at me without answering; he knew what was the matter with me.

"Just look what a night it is!" he called out from the parlor, where he had stopped by the open French window looking into the garden.

We joined him; and it really was such a night as I have never seen since. The full moon shone above the house and behind us, so that we could not see it, and half the shadow, thrown by the roof and pillars of the house and by the veranda awning, lay slanting and foreshortened on the gravel-path and the strip of turf beyond. Everything else was bright and saturated with the silver of the dew and the moonlight. The broad garden path, on one side of which the shadows of the dahlias and their supports lay aslant, all bright and cold, and shining on the inequalities of the gravel, ran on till it vanished in the mist. Through the trees the roof of the greenhouse shone bright, and a growing mist rose from the dell. The lilac bushes, already partly leafless, were all bright to the center. Each flower was distinguishable apart, and all were drenched with dew. In the avenues light and shade were so mingled that they looked, not like paths and trees but like transparent houses, swaying and moving. To our right, in the shadow of the house, everything was black, indistinguishable, and uncanny. But all the brighter for the surrounding darkness was the top of a poplar, with a fantastic crown of leaves, which for some strange reason remained there close to the house, towering into the bright light, instead of flying away into the dim distance, into the retreating dark blue of the sky.

"Let us go for a walk," I said.

Katya agreed, but said I must put on galoshes.

"I don't want them, Katya," I said; "Sergey Mikhaylych will give me his arm."

As if that would prevent me from wetting my feet! But to us three this seemed perfectly natural at the time. Though he never used to offer me his arm, I now took it of my own accord, and he saw nothing strange in it. We all went down from the veranda together. That whole world, that sky, that garden, that air, were different from those that I knew.

We were walking along an avenue, and it seemed to me, whenever I looked ahead, that we could go no farther in the same direction, that the world of the possible ended there, and that the whole scene must remain fixed for ever in its beauty. But we still moved on, and the magic wall kept parting to let us in; and still we found the familiar garden with trees and paths and withered leaves. And we were really walking along the paths, treading on patches of light and shade; and a withered leaf was really crackling under my foot, and a live twig brushing my face. And that was really he, walking steadily and slowly at my side, and carefully supporting my arm; and that was really Katya walking beside us with her creaking shoes. And that must be the moon in the sky, shining down on us through the motionless branches.

But at each step the magic wall closed up again behind us and in front, and I ceased to believe in the possibility of advancing father — I ceased to believe in the reality of it all.

"Oh, there's a frog!" cried Katya.

"Who said that? and why?" I thought. But then I realized it was Katya, and that she was afraid of frogs. Then I looked at the ground and saw a little frog which gave a jump and then stood still in front of me, while its tiny shadow was reflected on the shining clay of the path.

"You're not afraid of frogs, are you?" he asked.

I turned and looked at him. Just where we were there was a gap of one tree in the lime avenue, and I could see his face clearly — it was so handsome and so happy!

Though he had spoken of my fear of frogs, I knew that he meant to say, "I love you, my dear one!" "I love you, I love you" was repeated by his look, by his arm; by the light, the shadow, and the air all repeated the same words.

We had gone all round the garden. Katya's short steps had kept up with us, but now she was tired and out of breath. She said it was time to go in; and I felt very sorry for her. "Poor thing!" I thought; "why does not she feel as we do? why are we not all young and happy, like this night and like him and me?"

We went in, but it was a long time before he went away, though the cocks had crowed, and everyone in the house was asleep, and his horse, tethered under the window, snorted continually and stamped his hoof on the burdocks. Katya never reminded us of the hour, and we sat on talking of the merest trifles and not thinking of the time, till it was past two. The cocks were crowing for the third time and the dawn was breaking when he rode away. He said good by as usual and made no special allusion; but I knew that from that day he was mine, and that I should never lose him now. As soon as I had confessed to myself that I loved him, I took Katya into my confidence. She rejoiced in the news as was touched by my telling her; but she was actually able — poor thing! — to go to bed and sleep! For me, I walked for a long, long time about the veranda; then I went down to the garden where, recalling each word, each movement, I walked along the same avenues through which I had walked with him. I did not sleep at all that night, and saw sunrise and early dawn for the first time in my life. And never again did I see such a night and such a morning. "Only why does he not tell me plainly that he loves me?" I thought; "what makes him invent obstacles and call himself old, when all is so simple and so splendid? What makes him waste this golden time which may never return? Let him say "I love you" — say it in plain words; let him take my hand in his and ben over it and say "I love you". Let him blush and look down before me; and then I will tell him all. No! not tell him, but throw my arms round him and press close to him and weep." But then a thought came to me — "What if I am mistaken and he does not love me?"

I was startled by this fear — God knows where it might have led me. I recalled his embarrassment and mine, when I jumped down to him in the orchard; and my heart grew very heavy. Tears gushed from my eyes, and I began to pray. A strange thought occurred too me, calming me and bringing hope with it. I resolved to begin fasting on that day, to take the Communion on my birthday, and on that same day to be betrothed to him.

How this result would come to pass I had no idea; but from that moment I believed and felt sure it would be so. The dawn had fully come and the laborers were getting up when I went back to my room.

CHAPTER 4

The Fast of the Assumption falling in august, no one in the house was surprised by my intention of fasting.

During the whole of the week he never once came to see us; but, far from being surprised or vexed or made uneasy by his absence, I was glad of it — I did not expect him until my birthday. Each day during the week I got up early. while the horses were being harnessed, I walked in the garden alone, turning over in my mind the sins of the day before, and considering what I must do today, so as to be satisfied with my day and not spoil it by a singlesin. It seemed so easy to me then to abstain from sin altogether; only a trifling effort seemed necessary. When the horses came round, I got into the carriage with Katya or one of the maids, and we drove to the church two miles away. While entering the church, I always recalled the paryer for those who "come unto the Temple in the fear of God", and tried to get just that frame of mind when mounting the two grass-grown steps up to the building. At that hour there were not more than a dozen worshippers — household servants or peasant women keeping the Fast. They bowed to me, and I returned their bows with studied humility. Then, with what seemed to me a great effort of courage, I went myself and got candles from the man who kept them, an old soldier and an Elder; and I placed the candles before the icons. throught the central door of the altar-screen I could see the altar cloth which my mother had worked; on the screen were the two angels which had seemed so big to me when I was little, and the dove with a golden halo which had fascinated me long ago. Behind the choir stood the old batter font, where I had been christened myself and stood godmother to so many of the servants' children. the old priest came out, wearing a cope made of the pall that had covered my father's coffin, and began to read in the same voice that I had heard all my life — at services held in our house, at Sonya's christening, at memorial services for my father, and at my mother's funeral. The same old quavering voice of the deacon rose in the choir; and the same old woman, whom I could remember at every service in that church, crouched by the wall, fising her streaming eyes on an icon in the choir, pressing her folded fingers against her faded kerchief, and muttering with her toothless gums. And these objects were no longer merely curious to me, merely interesting from old recollections — each had become important and sacred in my eyes and seemed charged with profound meaning. I listened to each word of the prayrers and tried to suit my feeling to it; and if I failed to understand, I prayed silently that God would enlighten me, or made up a prayer of my own in place of what I had failed to catch. When the penitential prayers were repeated, I recalled my past life, and that innocent childish past seemed to me so black when compared to the present brightness of my soul, that I wept and was horrified at myself; but I felt too that all those sins would be forgiven, and that if my sins had been even greater, my repentance would be all the sweeter. At the end of the service when the priest said, "The blessing of the Lord be upon you!" I semed to feel an immediate sensation of physical well-being, of a mysterious light and warmth that instantly filled my heart. The service over, the priest came and asked me whether he should come to our house to say Mass, and what hour would suit me; and I thanked him for the suggestion, intended, as I thought, to please me, but said that I would come to church instead, walking or driving.

"Is that not too much trouble?" he asked. and I was at a loss for an answer, fearing to commit a sin of pride.

After the Mass, if Katya was not with me, I always sent the carriage home and walked back alone, bowing humbly to all who passed, and trying to find an opportunity of giving help or advice. I was eager to sacrifice myself for someone, to help in lifting a fallen cart, to rock a child's cradle, to give up the path to others by stepping into the mud. One evening I heard the bailiff report to Katya that Simon, one of our serfs, had come to beg some boards to make a coffin for his daughter, and a ruble to pay the priest for the funeral; the bailiff had given what he asked. "Are they as poor as that?" I asked. "Very poor, Miss," the bailiff answered; "they have no salt to their food." My heart ached to hear this, and yet I felt a kind of pleasure too. Pretending to katya that I was merely going for a walk, I ran upstairs, got out all my money (it was very little but it was all I had), crossed myself, and started off alone, through the veranda and the garden, on my way to Simon's hut. It stood at the end of the village, and no one saw me as I went up to the window, placed the money on the sill, and tapped on the pane. Someone came out, making the door creak, and hailed me; but I hurried home, cold and chaking with fear like a criminal. Katya asked where I had been and what was the matter with me; but I did not answer, and did not even understand what she was saying. Everything suddenly seemed to me so pety and insignificant. I locked myself up in my own room, and walked up and down alone for a long time, unable to do anything, unable to think, unable to understand my own feelings. I thought of the joy of the whole family, and of what they would say of their benefactor; and I felt sorry that I had not given them the money myself. I thought too of what Sergey Mikhaylych would say, if he knew what I had done; and I was glad to think that no one would ever find out. I was so happy, and I felt myself and everyone else so bad, and yet was so kindly disposed to myself and to all the world, that the thought of death came to me as a dream of happiness. I smiled and prayed and wept, and felt at that moment a burning passion of love for all the world, myself included. Between services I used to read the Gospel; and the book became more and more intelligible to me, and the story of that divine life simpler and more touching; and the depths of thought and feeling I found in studying it became more awful and impenetrable. On the other hand, how clear and simple everything seemed to me when I rose from the study of this book and looked again on life around me and reflected on it! It was so difficult, I felt, to lead a bad life, and so simple to love everyone and be loved. All were so kind and gentle to me; even sonya, whose lessons I had not broken off, was quite different — trying to understand and please me and not to vex me. Everyone treated me as I treated them. Thinking over my enemies, of whom I must ask pardon before confession, I could only remember one — one of our neighbors, a girl whom I had made fun of in company a year ago, and who had ceased to visit us. I wrote to her, confessing my fault and asking her forgiveness. she replied that she forgave me and wished me to forgive her. I cried for joy over her simple words, and saw in them, at the time, a deep and touching feeling. My old nurse cried, when I asked her to forgive me. "What makes them all so kind to me? what have I done to deserve their love?" I asked myself. Sergey Mikhaylych would come into my mind, and I thought for long about him. I could not help it, and I did not consider these thoughts sinful. But my thoughts of him were quite different from what they had been on the night when I first realized that I loved him: he seemed to me now like a second self, and became a part of every plan for the future. The inferiority which I had always felt in his presence had vanished entirely: I felt myself his equal and could understand him thoroughly from the moral elevation I had reached. What had seemed strange in him was now quite clear to me. Now I could see what he meant by saying to live for others was the only true happiness, and I agreed with him perfectly. I believed that our life together would be endlessly happy and untroubled. I looked forward, not to foreign tours or fashionable society or display, but to a quite different scene — a quiet family life in the country, with constant self-sacrifice, constant mutual love, and constant recognition in all things of the kind hand of Providence.

I carried out my plan of taking the Communion on my birthday. When I came back from church that day, my heart was so swelling with happiness that I was afraid of life, afraid of any feeling that might break in on that happiness. We had hardly left the carriage for the steps in front of the house, when there was a sound of wheels on the bridge, and I saw Sergey Mikhaylych drive up in his well-known trap. He congratulated me, and we went together to the parlour. Never since I had known him had I been so much at my ease with him and so self-possessed as on that morning. I felt in myself a whole new world out of his reach and beyond his comprehension. I was not consciousl of the slightest embarrassment in speaking to him. He must have understood the cause of this feeling; for he was tender and gentle beyond his wont and showed a kind of reverent consideration for me. When I made for the piano, he locked it and put the key in his pocket.

"Don't spoil your present mood," he said, "you have the sweetest of all music in your soul just now."

I was grateful for his words, and yet I was not quite pleased at his understanding too easily and clearly what ought to have been an exclusive secret in my heart. At dinner he said that he had come to congratulate me and also to say goodby; for he must go to Moscow tomorrow. FHe looked at Katya as he spoke; but then he stole a glance at me, and I saw that he was afraid he might detect signs of emotion on my face. But I was neither surprised nor agitated; I did not even ask whether he would be long away. I knew he would say this, and I knew that he would not go. How did I know? I cannot explain that to myself now; but on that memorable day it seemed that I knew everything that had been and that would be. It was like a delightful dream, when all that happenes seems to have happened already and to be quite familiar, and it will all happen over again, and one knows that it will happen.

He meant to go away immediately after dinner; but, as Katya was tired after church and went to lie down for a little, he had to wait until she woke up in order to say goodby to her. The sunshone into the drawing room, and we went out to the veranda. When we were seated, I began at once, quite calmly, the conversation that was bound to fix the fate of my heart. I began to speak,no sooner and no later, but at the very moment when we sat down, before our talk had taken any turn or color that might have hindered me from saying what I meant to say. I cannot tell myself where it came from — my coolness and determination and preciseness of expression. It was if something independent of my will was speaking through my lips. He sat opposite me with his elbows resting on the rails of the veranda; he pulled a lilac-branch towards him and stripped the leaves off it. When I began to speak, he let go the branch and leaned his head on one hand. His attitude might have shown either perfect calmness or strong emotion.

"Why are you going?" I asked, significantly, deliberately, and looking straight at him.

He did not answer at once.

"Business!" he muttered at last and dropped his eyes.

I realized how difficult he found it to lie to me, and in reply to such a frank question.

"Listen," I said; you know what today is to me, how important for many reasons. If I question you, it is not to show an interest in your doings (you know that I have become intimate with you and fond of you) — I ask you this question, because I must know the answer. Why are you going?"

"It is very hard for me to tell you the true reason," he said. "During this week I have thought much about you and about myself, and have decided that I must go. You understand why; and if you care for me, you will ask no questions." He put up a hand to rub his forehead and cover his eyes. "I find it very difficult . . . But you will understand."

My heart began to beat fast.

"I cannot understand you," I said; I cannot! you must tell me; in God's name and for the sake of this day tell me what you please, and I shall hear it with calmness," I said.

He changed his position, glanced at me, and again drew the lilac-twig towards him.

"Well!" he said, after a short silence and in a voice that tried in vain to seem steady, "it's a foolish business and impossible to put into words, and I feel the difficulty, but I will try to explain it to you," he added, frowning as if in bodily pain.

"Well?" I said.

"Just imagine the existence of a man — let us call him A— who has left youth far behind, and of a woman whom we may call B, who is young and happy and has seen nothing as yet of life or of the world. Family circumstances of various kinds brought them together, and he grew to love her as a daughter, and had no fear that his love would change its nature."

He stopped, but I did not interrupt him.

"But he forgot that B was so young, that life was still all a May-game to her," he went on with a sudden swiftness and determination and without looking at me, "and that it was easy to fall in love with her in a different way, and that this would amuse her. He made a mistake and was suddenly aware of another feeling, as heavy as remorse, making its way into his heart, and he was afraid. He was afraid that their old friendly relations would be destroyed, and he made up his mind to go away before that happened." As he said this, he began again to rub his eyes with a pretence of indifference, and to close them.

"Why was he afraid to love differently?" I asked very low; but I restrained my emotion and spokein an even voice. He evidently thought that I was not serious; for he answered as if he were hurt.

"You are young, and I am not young. You want amusement, and I want something different. Amuse yourself, if you like, but not with me. If you do, I shall take it seriously; and then I shall be unhappy, and you will repent. That is what A said," he added; "however, this is all nonsense; but you understand why I am going. And don't let us continue this conversation. Please not!"

"No! no!" I said, "we must continue it," and tears began to tremble in my voice. "Did he lover her, or not?"

He did not answer.

"If he did not love her, why did he treat her as a child and pretend to love her?" I asked.

"Yes, A behaved badly," he interrupted me quickly; "but it all came to an end and they parted friends."

"This is horrible! Is there no other ending?" I said with a great effort and then felt afraid of what I had said.

"Yes, there is," he said, showing a face full of emotion and looking straight at me. "There are two different endings. But, for God's sake, listen to me quietly and don't interrupt. Some say" — here he stood up and smiled with a smile that was heavy with pain — "some say that A went off his head, fell passionately in love with B, and told her so. But she only laughed. To her it was all a jest, but to him a matter of life and death."

I shuddered and tried to interrupt him — tried to say that he must not dare to speak for me; but he checked me, laying his hand on mine.

"Wait!" he said, and his voice shook. "The other story is that she took pity on him, and fancied, poor child, from her ignorance of the world, that she really could love hiim, and so consented to be his wife. And he, in his madness, believed it — believed that his whole life could begin anew; but she saw herself that she had deceived him and that he had deceived her. . . . But let us drop the subject finally," he ended, clearly unable to say more; and then he began to walk up and down in silence before me.

Thought he had asked that subject should be dropped, I saw that his whole soul was hanging on my answer. I tried to speak, but the pain at my heart kept me dumb. I glanced at him — he was pale and his lower lip trembled. I felt sorry for him. with a sudden effort I broke the bonds of silence which had held me fast, and began to speak in a low inward voice, which I feared would break every moment.

"There is a third ending to the story," I said, and then paused, but he said nothing; "the third ending is that he did not love her, but hurt her, hurt her, and thought that he was right; and he left her and was actually proud of himself. You have been pretending, not I; I have loved you since the first day we met, loved you," I repeated, and at the word "loved" my low inward voice changed, without intention of mine, to a wild cry which frightened me myself.

He stood pale before me, his lip trembled more and more violently, and two tears came out upon his cheeks.

"It is wrong!" I almost screamed, feeling that I was choking with angry unshed tears. "Why do you do it?" I cried and got up to leave him.

But he would not let me go. His head was resting on my knees, his lips were kissing my still trembling hands, and his tears were wetting them. "My God! if I had only known!" he whispered.

"why? why?" I kept on repeating, but in my heart there was happiness, happiness which had now come back, after so nearly departing for ever.

Five minutes later Sonya was rushing upstairs to Katya and proclaiming all over the house that Masha intended to marry Sergey Mikhaylych.

CHAPTER 5

There were no reasons for putting off our wedding, and neither he nor I wished for delay. Katya, it is true, thought we ought to go to Moscow, to buy and order wedding clothes; and his mother tried to insist that, before the wedding, he must set up a new carriage, but new furniture, and repaper the whole house. But we two together carried our point, that all these things, if they were really indispensable, should be done afterwards, and that we should be married within a fortnight after my birthday, quietly, without wedding clothes, with a party, without best men and supper and champagne, and all the other conventional features of a wedding. He told me how dissatisfied his mother was that there should be no band, no mountain of luggage, no renovation of the whole house — so unlike her own marriage which had cost thirty thousand rubles; and he told of the solemn and secret confabulations which she held in her store room with her housekeeper, Maryushka, rummaging the chests and discussing carpets, curtains, and salvers as indispensable conditions of our happiness. At our house Katya did just the same with my old nurse, Kuzminichna. It was impossible to treat the matter lightly with Katya. She was firmly convinced that he and I, when discussing our future, were merely talking the sentimental nonsense natural to people in our position; and that our real future happiness depended on the hemming of table cloths and napkins and the proper cutting out and stitching of underclothing. Several times a day secret information passed between the two houses, to communicate what was going forward in each; and though the external relations between Katya and his mother were most affectionate, yet a slightly hostile though very subtle diplomacy was already perceptible in their dealings. I now became more intimate with Tatyana Semyonovna, the mother of Sergey Mikhaylych, an old-fashioned lady, strict and formal in the management of her household. Her son loved her, and not merely because she was his mother: he thought her the best, cleverest, kindest, and most affectionate woman in the world. She was always kind to us and to me especially, and was glad that her son should be getting married; but when I was with her after our engagement, I always felt that she wished me to understand that, in her opinion, her son might have looked higher, and that it would be as well for me to keep that in mind. I understood her meaning perfectly and thought her quite right.

During that fortnight he and I met every day. He came to dinner regularly and stayed on till midnight. But though he said — and I knew he was speaking the truth — that he had no life apart from me, yet he never spent the whole day with me, and tried to go on with his ordinary occupations. Our outward relations remained unchanged to the very day of our marriage: we went on saying "you" and not "thou" to each other; he did not even kiss my hand; he did not seek, but even avoided, opportunities of being alone with me. It was as if he feared to yield to the harmful excess of tenderness he felt. I don't know which of us had changed; but I now felt myself entirely his equal; I no longer found in him the pretence of simplicity which had displeased me earlier; and I often delighted to see in him, not a grown man inspiring respect and awe but a loving and wildly happy child. "How mistaken I was about him!" I often thought; "he is just such another human being as myself!" It seemed to me now, that his whole character was before me and that I thoroughly understood it. And how simple was every feature of his character, and how congenial to my own! Even his plans for our future life together were just my plans, only more clearly and better expressed in his words.

The weather was bad just then, and we spent most of our time indoors. The corner between the piano and the window was the scene of our best intimate talks. The candle light was reflected on the blackness of the window near us; from time to time drops struck the glistening pane and rolled down. The rain pattered on the roof; the water splashed in a puddle under the spout; it felt damp near the window; but our corner seemed all the brighter and warmer and happier for that.

"Do you know, there is something I have long wished to say to you," he began one night when we were sitting up late in our corner; "I was thinking of it all the time you were playing."

"Don't say it, I know all about it," I replied.

"All right! mum's the word!"

"No! what is it?" I asked.

"Well, it is this. You remember the story I told you about A and B?"

"I should just think I did! What a stupid story! Lucky that it ended as it did!"

"Yes. I was very near destroying my happiness by my own act. You saved me. But the main thing is that I was always telling lies then, and I'm ashamed of it, and I want to have my say out now."

"Please don't! you really mustn't!"

"Don't be frightened," he said, smiling. "I only want to justify myself. When I began then, I meant to argue."

"It is always a mistake to argue," I said.

"Yes, I argued wrong. After all my disappointments and mistakes in life, I told myself firmly when I came to the country this year, that love was no more for me, and that all I had to do was to grow old decently. So for a long time, I was unable to clear up my feeling towards you, or to make out where it might lead me. I hoped, and I didn't hope: at one time I thought you were trifling with me; at another I felt sure of you but could not decide what to do. But after that evening, you remember when we walked in the garden at night, I got alarmed: the present happiness seemed too great to be real. What if I allowed myself to hope and then failed? But of course I was thinking only of myself, for I am disgustingly selfish."

He stopped and looked at me.

"But it was not all nonsense that I said then. It was possible and right for me to have fears. I take so much from you and can give so little. You are still a child, a bud that has yet to open; you have never been in love before, and I . . ."

"Yes, do tell me the truth . . . ." I began, and then stopped, afraid of his answer. "No, never mind," I added.

"Have I been in love before? is that it?" he said, guessing my thoughts at once. "That I can tell you. No, never before — nothing a t all like what I feel now." But a sudden painful recollection seemed to flash across his mind. "No," he said sadly; "in this too I need your compassion, in order to have the right to love you. Well, was I not bound to think twice before saying that I loved you? What do I give you? love, no doubt."

"And is that little?" I asked, looking him in the face.

"Yes, my dear, it is little to give you," he continued; "you have youth and beauty. I often lie awake at night from happiness, and all the time I think of our future life together. I have lived through much, and now I think I have found what is needed for happiness. A quiet secluded life in the country, with the possibility of being useful to people to whom it is easy to do good, and who are not accustomed to have it done to them; then work which one hopes may be of some use; then rest, nature, books, music, love for one's neighbor — such is my idea of happiness. And then, on the top of all that, you for a mate, and children perhaps — what more can the hear of man desire?"

"It should be enough," I said.

"Enough for me whose youth is over," he went on, "but not for you. Life is still before you, and you will perhaps seek happiness, and perhaps find it, in something different. You think now that this is happiness, because you love me."

"You are wrong," I said; "I have always desired just that quiet domestic life and prized it. And you only say just what I have thought."

He smiled.

"So you think, my dear; but that is not enough for you. You have youth and beauty," he repeated thoughtfully.

But I was angry because he disbelieved me and seemed to cast my youth and beauty in my teeth.

"Why do you love me then?" I asked angrily; "for my youth or for myself?"

"I don't know, but I love you," he answered, looking at me with his attentive and attractive gaze.

I did not reply and involuntarily looked into his eyes. Suddenly a strange thing happened to me: first I ceased to see what was around me; then his face seemed to vanish till only the eyes were left, shining over against mine; next the eyes seemed to be in my own head, and then all became confused — I could see nothing and was forced to shut my eyes, in order to break loose from the feeling of pleasure and fear which his gaze was producing in me . . .

The day before our wedding day, the weather cleared up towards evening. The rains which had begun in summer gave place to clear weather, and we had our first autumn evening, bright and cold. It was a wet, cold, shining world, and the garden showed for the first time the spaciousness and color and bareness of autumn. the sky was clear, cold, and pale. I went to bed happy in the thought that tomorrow, our wedding day, would be fine. I awoke with the sun, and the thought that this very day . . . seemed alarming and surprising. I went out into the garden. the sun had just risen and shone fitfully through the meager yellow leaves of the lime avenue. The path was strewn with rustling leaves, clusters of mountain ash berries hung red and wrinkled on the boughs, with a sprinkling of frost-bitten crumpled leaves; the dahlias were black and wrinkled. the first rime lay like silver on the pale green of the grass and on the broken burdock plants round the house. In the clear cold sky there was not, and could not be, a single cloud.

"Can it possibly be today?" I asked myself, incredulous of my own happiness. "Is it possible that I shall wake tomorrow, not here but in that strange house with the pillars? Is it possible that I shall never again wait for his coming and meet him, and sit up late with Katya to talk about him? Shall I never sit with him beside the piano in our drawing room? never see him off and feel uneasy about him on dark nights?" But I remembered that he promised yesterday to pay a last visit, and that Katya had insisted on my trying on my wedding dress, and had said "For tomorrow". I believed for a moment that it was all real, and then doubted again. "Can it be that after today I shall be living there with a mother-inlaw, without Nadezhda or Grigori or Katya? Shall I go to bed without kissing my old nurse good night and hearing her say, while she signs me with the cross from old custom, "Good night, Miss"? Shall I never again teach Sonya and play with her and knock through the wall to her in the morning and hear her hearty laugh? Shall I become from today someone that I myself do not know? and is a new world, that will realize my hopes and desires, opening before me? and will that new world last for ever?" alone with these thoughts I was depressed and impatient for his arrival. He cam early, and it required his presence to convince me that I should really be his wife that very day, and the prospect ceased to frighten me.

Before dinner we walked to our church, to attend a memorial service for my father.

"If only he were living now!" I thought as we were returning and I leant silently on the arm of him who had been the dearest friend of the object of my thoughts. During the service, while I pressed my forehead against the cold stone of the chapel floor, I called up my father so vividly; I was so convinced that he understood me and approved my choice, that I felt as if his spirit were still hovering over us and blessing me. And my recollections and hopes, my joy and sadness, made up one solemn and satisfied feeling which was in harmony with the fresh still air, the silence, the bare fields and pale sky, from which the bright but powerless rays, trying in vain to burn my cheek, fell over all the landscape. My companion seemed to understand and share my feeling. He walked slowly and silently; and his face, at which I glanced from time to time, expressed the same serious mood between joy and sorrow which I shared with nature.

Suddenly he turned to me, and I saw that he intended to speak. "Suppose he starts some other subject than that which is in my mind?" I thought. But he began to speak of my father and did not even name him.

"He once said to me in just, "you should marry my Masha"," he began.

"He would have been happy now," I answered, pressing closer the arm which held mine.

"You were a child then," he went on, looking into my eyes; "I loved those eyes and used to kiss them only because they were like his, never thinking they would be so dear to me for their own sake. I used to call you Masha then."

"I want you to say thou' to me," I said.

"I was just going to," he answered; "I feel for the first time that thou art entirely mine;" and his calm happy gaze that drew me to him rested on me.

We went on along the foot path over the beaten and trampled stubble; our voices and footsteps were the only sounds. On one side the brownish stubble stretched over a hollow to a distant leafless wood; across it at some distance a peasant was noiselessly ploughing a black strip which grew wider and wider. A drove of horses scattered under the hill seemed close to us. On the other side, as far as the garden and our house peeping through the trees, a field of winter corn, thawed by the sun, showed black with occasional patches of green. The winter sun shone over everything, and everything was covered with long gossamer spider's webs, which floated in the air round us, lay on the frost-dried stubble, and got into our eyes and hair and clothes. When we spoke, the sound of our voices hung in the motionless air above us, as if we two were alone in the whole world — alone under that azure vault, in which the beams of the winter sun played and flashed without scorching.

I too wished to say "thou" to him, but I felt ashamed.

"Why dost thou walk so fast?" I said quickly and almost in a whisper; I could not help blushing.

He slackened his pace, and the gaze he turned on me was even more affectionate, gay, and happy.

At home we found that his mother and the inevitable guests had arrived already, and I was never alone with him again till we came out of church to drive to Nikolskoe.

The church was nearly empty: I just caught a glimpse of his mother standing up straight on a mat by the choir and of Katya wearing a cap with purple ribbons and with tears on her cheeks, and of two or three of our servants looking curiously at me. I did not look at him, but felt his presence there beside me. I attended to the words of the prayers and repeated them, but they found no echo in my heart. Unable to pray, I looked listlessly at the icons, the candles, the embroidered cross on the priest's cope, the screen, and the window, and took nothing in. I only felt that something strange was being done to me. At last the priest turned to us with the cross in his hand, congratulated us, and said, "I christened you and by God's mercy have lived to marry you." Katya and his mother kissed us, and Grigori's voice was heard, calling up the carriage. But I was only frightened and disappointed: all was over, but nothing extraordinary, nothing worthy of the Sacrament I had just received, had taken place in myself. He and I exchanged kisses, but the kiss seemed strange and not expressive of our feeling. "Is this all?" I thought. We went out of church, the sound of wheels reverberated under the vaulted roof, the fresh air blew on my face, he put on his hat and handed me into the carriage. Through the window I could see a frosty moon with a halo round it. He sat down beside me and shut the door after him. I felt a sudden pang. The assurance of his proceedings seemed to me insulting. Katya called out that I should put something on my head; the wheels rumbled on the stone and then moved along the soft road, and we were off. Huddling in a corner, I looked out at the distant fields and the road flying past in the cold glitter of the moon. Without looking at him, I felt his presence beside me. "Is this all I have got from the moment, of which I expected so much?" I thought; and still it seemed humiliating and insulting to be sitting alone with him, and so close. I turned to him, intending to speak; but the words would not come, as if my love had vanished, giving place to a feeling of mortification and alarm.

"Till this moment I did not believe it was possible," he said in a low voice in answer to my look.

"But I am afraid somehow," I said.

"Afraid of me, my dear?" he said, taking my hand and bending over it.

My hand lay lifeless in his, and the cold at my heart was painful.

"Yes," I whispered.

But at that moment my heart began to beat faster, my hand trembled and pressed his, I grew hot, my eyes sought his in the half darkness, and all at once I felt that I did not fear him, that this fear was love — a new love still more tender and stronger than the old. I felt that I was wholly his, and that I was happy in his power over me.

****

PART II

CHAPTER 1

Days, weeks, two whole months of seclusion in the country slipped by unnoticed, as we thought then; and yet those two months comprised feelings, emotions, and happiness, sufficient for a lifetime. Our plans for the regulation of our life in the country were not carried out at all in the way that we expected; but the reality was not inferior to our ideal. There was none of that hard work, performance of duty, self-sacrifice, and life for others, which I had pictured to myself before our marriage; there was, on the contrary, merely a selfish feeling of love for one another, a wish to be loved, a constant causeless gaiety and entire oblivion of all the world. It is true that my husband sometimes went to his study to work, or drove to town on business, or walked about attending to the management of the estate; but I saw what it cost him to tear himself away from me. He confessed later that every occupation, in my absence, seemed to him mere nonsense in which it was impossible to take any interest. It was just the same with me. If I read, or played the piano, or passed my time with his mother, or taught in the school, I did so only because each of these occupations was connected with him and won his approval; but whenever the thought of him was not associated with any duty, my hands fell by my sides and it seemed to me absurd to think that any thing existed apart from him. Perhaps it was a wrong and selfish feeling, but it gave me happiness and lifted me high above all the world. He alone existed on earth for me, and I considered him the best and most faultless man in the world; so that I could not live for anything else than for him, and my one object was to realize his conception of me. And in his eyes I was the first and most excellent woman in the world, the possessor of all possible virtues; and I strove to be that woman in the opinion of the first and best of men.

He came to my room one day while I was praying. I looked round at him and went on with my prayers. Not wishing to interrupt me, he sat down at a table and opened a book. But I thought he was looking at me and looked round myself. He smiled, I laughed, and had to stop my prayers.

"Have you prayed already?" I asked.

"Yes. But you go; I'll go away."

"You do say your prayers, I hope?"

He made no answer and was about to leave the room when I stopped him.

"Darling, for my sake, please repeat the prayers with me!" He stood up beside me, dropped his arms awkwardly, and began, with a serious face and some hesitation. Occasionally he turned towards me, seeking signs of approval and aid in my face.

When he came to an end, I laughed and embraced him.

"I feel just as if I were ten! And you do it all!" he said, blushing and kissing my hands.

Our house was one of those old-fashioned country houses in which several generations have passed their lives together under one roof, respecting and loving one another. It was all redolent of good sound family traditions, which as soon as I entered it seemed to become mine too. The management of the household was carried on by Tatyana Semyonovna, my mother-inlaw, on old-fashioned lines. Of grace and beauty there was not much; but, from the servants down to the furniture and food, there was abundance of everything, and a general cleanliness, solidity, and order, which inspired respect. The drawing room furniture was arranged symmetrically; there were portraits on the walls, and the floor was covered with home-made carpets and mats. In the morning-room there was an old piano, with chiffoniers of two different patterns, sofas, and little carved tables with bronze ornaments. My sitting room, specially arranged by Tatyana Semyonovna, contained the best furniture in the house, of many styles and periods, including an old pierglass, which I was frightened to look into at first, but came to value as an old friend. Though Tatyana Semyonovna's voice was never heard, the whole household went like a clock. The number of servants was far too large (they all wore soft boots with no heels, because Tatyana Semyonovna had an intense dislike for stamping heels and creaking soles); but they all seemed proud of their calling, trembled before their old mistress, treated my husband and me with an affectionate air of patronage, and performed their duties, to all appearance, with extreme satisfaction. Every Saturday the floors were scoured and the carpets beaten without fail; on the first of every month there was a religious service in the house and holy water was sprinkled; on Tatyana Semyonovna's name day and on her son's (and on mine too, beginning from that autumn) an entertainment was regularly provided for the whole neighborhood. and all this had gone on without a break ever since the beginning of Tatyana Semyonovna's life.

My husband took no part in the household management, he attended only to the farm-work and the laborers, and gave much time to this. Even in winter he got up so early that I often woke to find him gone. He generally came back for early tea, which we drank alone together; and at that time, when the worries and vexations of the farm were over, he was almost always in that state of high spirits which we called "wild ecstasy". I often made him tell me what he had been doing in the morning, and he gave such absurd accounts that we both laughed till we cried. Sometimes I insisted on a serious account, and he gave it, restraining a smile. I watched his eyes and moving lips and took nothing in: the sight of him and the sound of his voice was pleasure enough.

"Well, what have I been saying? repeat it," he would sometimes say. But I could repeat nothing. It seemed so absurd that he should talk to me of any other subject than ourselves. As if it mattered in the least what went on in the world outside! It was at a much later time that I began to some extent to understand and take an interest in his occupations. Tatyana Semyonovna never appeared before dinner: she breakfasted alone and said good morning to us by deputy. In our exclusive little world of frantic happiness a voice form the staid orderly region in which she dwelt was quite startling: I often lost self-control and could only laugh without speaking, when the maid stood before me with folded hands and made her formal report: "The mistress bade me inquire how you slept after your walk yesterday evening; and about her I was to report that she had pain in her side all night, and a stupid dog barked in the village and kept her awake; and also I was to ask how you liked the bread this morning, and to tell you that it was not Taras who baked today, but Nikolashka who was trying his hand for the first time; and she says his baking is not at all bad, especially the cracknesl: but the tea-rusks were over-baked." Before dinner we saw little of each other: he wrote or went out again while I played the piano or read; but at four o'clock we all met in the drawing room before dinner. Tatyana Semyonovna sailed out of her own room, and certain poor and pious maiden ladies, of whom there were always two or three living in the house, made their appearance also. Every day without fail my husband by old habit offered his arm to his mother, to take her in to dinner; but she insisted that I should take the other, so that every day, without fail, we stuck in the doors and got in each other's way. She also presided at dinner, where the conversation, if rather solemn, was polite and sensible. The commonplace talk between my husband and me was a pleasant interruption to the formality of those entertainments. Sometimes there were squabbles between mother and son and they bantered one another; and I especially enjoyed the scenes, because they were the best proof of the strong and tender love which united the two. after dinner Tatyana Semyonovna went to the parlor, where she sat in an armchair and ground her snuff or cut the leaves of new books, while we read aloud or went off to the piano in the morning room. We read much together at this time, but music was our favorite and best enjoyment, always evoking fresh chords in our hearts and as it were revealing each afresh to the other. While I played his favorite pieces, he sat on a distant sofa where I could hardly see him. He was ashamed to betray the impression produced on him by the music; but often, when he was not expecting it, I rose from the piano, went up to him, and tried to detect on his face signs of emotion — the unnatural brightness and moistness of the eyes, which he tried in vain to conceal. Tatyana Semyonovna, though she often wanted to take a look at us there, was also anxious to put no constraint upon us. So she always passed through the room with an air of indifference and a pretence of being busy; but I knew that she had no real reason for going to her room and returning so soon. In the evening I poured out tea in the large drawing room, and all the household met again. This solemn ceremony of distributing cups and glasses before the solemnly shining samovar made me nervous for a long time. I felt myself still unworthy of such a distinction, too young and frivolous to turn the tap of such a big samovar, to put glasses on Nikita's salver, saying "For Peter Ivanovich", "For Marya Minichna", to ask "Is it sweet enough?" and to leave out limps of sugar for Nurse and other deserving persons. "Capital! capital! Just like a grown-up person!" was a frequent comment from my husband, which only increased my confusion.

After tea Tatyana Semyonovna played patience or listened to Marya Minichna telling fortunes by the cards. Then she kissed us both and signed us with the cross, and we went off to our own rooms. But we generally sat up together till midnight, and that was our best and pleasantest time. He told me stories of his past life; we made plans and sometimes even talked philosophy; but we tried always to speak low, for fear we should be heard upstairs and reported to Tatyana Semyonovna, who insisted on our going to bed early. Sometimes we grew hungry; and then we stole off to the pantry, secured a cold supper by the good offices of Nikita, and ate it in my sitting room by the light of one candle. He and I lived like strangers in that big old house, where the uncompromising spirit of the past and of Tatyana Semyonovna ruled supreme. Not she only, but the servants, the old ladies, the furniture, even the pictures, inspired me with respect and a little alarm, and made me feel that he and I were a little out of place in that house and must always be very careful and cautious in our doings. Thinking it over now, I see that many things — the pressure of that unvarying routine, and that crowd of idle and inquisitive servants — were uncomfortable and oppressive; but at the time that very constraint made our love for one another still keener. Not I only, but he also, never grumbled openly at anything; on the contrary he shut his eyes to what was amiss. Dmitriy Sidorov, one of the footmen, was a great smoker; and regularly every day, when we two were in the morning room after dinner, he went to my husband's study to take tobacco from the jar; and it was a sight to see Sergey Mikhaylych creeping on tiptoe to me with a face between delight and terror, and a wink and a warning forefinger, while he pointed at Dmitriy Sidorov, who was quite unconscious of being watched. Then, when Dmitriy Sidorov had gone away without having seen us, in his joy that all had passed off successfully, he declared (as he did on every other occasion) that I was a darling, and kissed me. At times his calm connivance and apparent indifference to everything annoyed me, and I took it for weakness, never noticing that I acted in the same way myself. "It's like a child who dares not show his will," I thought.

"My dear! my dear!" he said once when I told him that his weakness surprised me; "how can a man, as happy as I am, be dissatisfied with anything? Better to give way myself than to put compulsion on others; of that I have long been convinced. There is no condition in which one cannot be happy; but our life is such bliss! I simply cannot be angry; to me now nothing seems bad, but only pitiful and amusing. Above all — le mieux est l'ennemi du bien. Will you believe it, when I hear a ring at the bell, or receive a letter, or even wake up in the morning, I'm frightened. Life must go on, something may change; and nothing can be better than the present."

I believed him but did not understand him. I was happy; but I took that as a matter of course, the invariable experience of people in our position, and believed that there was somewhere, I knew not where, a different happiness, not greater but different.

So two months went by and winter came with its cold and snow; and, in spite of his company, I began to feel lonely, that life was repeating itself, that there was nothing new either in him or in myself, and that we were merely going back to what had been before. He began to give more time to business which kept him away from me, and my old feeling returned, that there was a special department of his mind into which he was unwilling to admit me. His unbroken calmness provoked me. I loved him as much as ever and was as happy as ever in his love; but my love, instead of increasing, stood still; and another new and disquieting sensation began to creep into my heart. To love him was not enough for me after the happiness I had felt in falling in love. I wanted movement and not a calm course of existence. I wanted excitement and danger and the chance to sacrifice myself for my love. I felt in myself a superabundance of energy which found no outlet in our quiet life. I had fits of depression which I was ashamed of and tried to conceal from him, and fits of excessive tenderness and high spirits which alarmed him. He realized my state of mind before I did, and proposed a visit to Petersburg; but I begged him to give this up and not to change our manner of life or spoil our happiness. Happy indeed I was; but I was tormented by the thought that this happiness cost me no effort and no sacrifice, though I was even painfully conscious of my power to fact both. I loved him and saw that I was all in all to him; but I wanted everyone to see our love; I wanted to love him in spite of obstacles. My mind, and even my senses, were fully occupied; but there was another feeling of youth and craving for movement, which found no satisfaction in our quiet life. What made him say that, whenever I liked, we could go to town? Had he not said so I might have realized that my uncomfortable feelings were my own fault and dangerous nonsense, and that the sacrifice I desired was there before me, in the task of overcoming these feelings. I was haunted by the thought that I could escape from depression by a mere change from the country; and at the same time I felt ashamed and sorry to tear him away, out of selfish motives, from all he cared for. So time went on, the snow grew deeper, and there we remained together, all alone and just the same as before, while outside I knew there was noise and glitter and excitement, and hosts of people suffering or rejoicing without one thought of us and our remote existence. I suffered most from the feeling that custom was daily petrifying our lives into one fixed shape, that our minds were losing their freedom and becoming enslaved to the steady passionless course of time. The morning always found us cheerful; we were polite at dinner, and affectionate in the evening. "It is all right," I thought, "to do good to others and lead upright lives, as he says; but there is time for that later; and there are other things, for which the time is now or never." I wanted, not what I had got, but a life of struggle; I wanted feeling to be the guide of life, and not life to guide feeling. If only I could go with him to the edge of a precipice and say, "One step, and I shall fall over — one movement, and I shall be lost!" then, pale with fear, he would catch me in his strong arms and hold me over the edge till my blood froze, and then carry me off whither he pleased.

This state of feeling even affected my health, and I began to suffer from nerves. One morning I was worse than usual. He had come beck from the estate office out of sorts, which was a rare thing with him. I noticed it at once and asked what was the matter. He would not tell me and said it was of no importance. I found out afterwards that the police inspector, out of spite against my husband, was summoning our peasants, making illegal demands on them, and using threats to them. My husband could not swallow this at once; he could not feel it merely "pitiful and amusing". He was provoked, and therefore unwilling to speak of it to me. But it seemed to me that he did not wish to speak to about it because he considered me a mere child, incapable of understanding his concerns. I turned from him and said no more. I then told the servant to ask Marya Minichna, who was staying in the house, to join us at breakfast. I ate my breakfast very fast and took her to the morning room where I began to talk loudly to her about some trifle which did not interest me in he least. He walked about the room, glancing at us from time to time. This made me more and more inclined to talk and even to laugh; all that I said myself, and all that Marya Minichna said, seemed to me laughable. Without a word to me he went off to his study and shut the door behind him. When I ceased to hear him, all my high spirits vanished at once; indeed Marya Minichna was surprised and asked what was the matter. I sat down on a sofa without answering, and felt ready to cry. "What has he got on his mind?" I wondered; "some trifle which he thinks important; but, if he tried to tell it me, I should soon show him it was mere nonsense. But he must needs think that I won't understand, must humiliate me by his majestic composure, and always be in the right as against me. But I too am in the right when I find things tiresome and trivial," I reflected; "and I do well to want an active life rather than to stagnate in one spot and feel life flowing past me. I want to move forward, to have some new experience every day and every hour, whereas he wants to stand still and to keep me standing beside him. And how easy it would be for him to gratify me! He need not take me to town; he need only be like me and not put compulsion on himself and regulate his feelings, but live simply. That is the advice he gives me, but he is not simple himself. That is what is the matter."

I felt the tears rising and knew that I was irritated with him. My irritation frightened me, and I went to his study. He was sitting at the table, writing. Hearing my step, he looked up for a moment and then went on writing; he seemed calm and unconcerned. His look vexed me: instead of going up to him, I stood beside his writing table, opened a book, and began to look at it. He broke off his writing again and looked at me.

"Masha, are you out of sorts?" he asked.

I replied with a cold look, as much as to say, "You are very polite, but what is the use of asking?" He shook his head and smiled with a tender timid air; but his smile, for the first time, drew no answering smile from me.

"What happened to you today?" I asked; "why did you not tell me?"

"Nothing much — a trifling nuisance," he said. "But I might tell you now. Two of our serfs went off to the town . . ."

But I would not let him go on.

"Why would you not tell me, when I asked you at breakfast?:

"I was angry then and should have said something foolish."

"I wished to know then."

"Why?"

"Why do you suppose that I can never help you in anything?"

"Not help me!" he said, dropping his pen. "Why, I believe that without you I could not live. You not only help me in everything I do, but you do it yourself. You are very wide of the mark," he said, and laughed. "My life depends on you. I am pleased with things, only because you are there, because I need you . . ."

"Yes, I know; I am a delightful child who must be humored and kept quiet," I said in a voice that astonished him, so that he looked up as if this was a new experience; "but I don't want to be quiet and calm; that is more in your line, and too much in your line," I added.

"Well," he began quickly, interrupting me and evidently afraid to let me continue, "when I tell you the facts, I should like to know your opinion."

"I don't want to hear them now," I answered. I did want to hear the story, but I found it so pleasant to break down his composure. "I don't want to play at life," I said, "but to live, as you do yourself."

His face, which reflected every feeling so quickly and so vividly, now expressed pain and intense attention.

"I want to share your life, to . . .," but I could not go on — his face showed such deep distress. He was silent for a moment.

"But what part of my life do you not share?" he asked; "is it because I, and not you, have to bother with the inspector and with tipsy laborers?"

"That's not the only thing," I said.

"For God's sake try to understand me, my dear!" he cried. "I know that excitement is always painful; I have learnt that from the experience of life. I love you, and I can't but wish to save you from excitement. My life consists of my love for you; so you should not make life impossible for me."

"You are always in the right," I said without looking at him.

I was vexed again by his calmness and coolness while I was conscious of annoyance and some feeling akin to penitence.

"Masha, what is the matter?" he asked. "The question is not, which of us is in the right — not at all; but rather, what grievance have you against me? Take time before you answer, and tell me all that is in your mind. You are dissatisfied with me: and you are, no doubt, right; but let me understand what I have done wrong."

But how could I put my feeling into words? That he understood me at once, that I again stood before him like a child, that I could do nothing without his understanding and foreseeing it — all this only increased my agitation.

"I have no complaint to make of you," I said; "I am merely bored and want not to be bored. But you say that it can't be helped, and, as always, you are right."

I looked at him as I spoke. I had gained my object: his calmness had disappeared, and I read fear and pain in his face.

"Masha," he began in a low troubled voice, "this is no mere trifle: the happiness of our lives is at stake. Please hear me out without answering. why do you wish to torment me?"

But I interrupted him.

"Oh, I know you will turn out to be right. Words are useless; of course you are right." I spoke coldly, as if some evil spirit were speaking with my voice.

"If you only knew what you are doing!" he said, and his voice shook.

I burst out crying and felt relieved. He sat down beside me and said nothing. I felt sorry for him, ashamed of myself, and annoyed at what I had done. I avoided looking at him. I felt that any look from him at that moment must express severity or perplexity. At last I looked up and saw his eyes: they were fixed on me with a tender gentle expression that seemed to ask for pardon. I caught his hand and said,

"Forgive me! I don't know myself what I have been saying."

"But I do; and you spoke the truth."

"What do you mean?" I asked.

"That we must go to Petersburg," he said; "there is nothing for us to do here just now."

"As you please," I said.

He took me in his arms and kissed me.

"You must forgive me," he said; "for I am to blame."

That evening I played to him for a long time, while he walked about the room. He had a habit of muttering to himself; and when I asked him what he was muttering, he always thought for a moment and then told me exactly what it was. It was generally verse, and sometimes mere nonsense, but I could always judge of his mood by it. When I asked him now, he stood still, thought an instant, and then repeated two lines from Lermontov:

He is his madness prays for storms,

And dreams that storms will bring him peace.

"He is really more than human," I thought; "he knows everything. How can one help loving him?"

I got up, took his arm, and began to walk up and down with him, trying to keep step.

"Well?" he asked, smiling and looking at me.

"All right," I whispered. And then a sudden fit of merriment came over us both: our eyes laughed, we took longer and longer steps, and rose higher and higher on tiptoe. Prancing in this manner, to the profound dissatisfaction of the butler and astonishment of my mother-inlaw, who was playing patience in the parlor, we proceeded through the house till we reached the dining room; there we stopped, looked at one another, and burst out laughing.

A fortnight later, before Christmas, we were in Petersburg.

The journey to Petersburg, a week in Moscow, visits to my own relations and my husband's, settling down in our new quarters, travel, new towns and new faces — all this passed before me like a dream. It was all so new, various, and delightful, so warmly and brightly lighted up by his presence and his live, that our quiet life in the country seemed to me something very remote and unimportant. I had expected to find people in society proud and cold; but to my great surprise, I was received everywhere with unfeigned cordiality and pleasure, not only by relations, but also by strangers. I seemed to be the one object of their thoughts, and my arrival the one thing they wanted, to complete their happiness. I was surprised too to discover in what seemed to me the very best society a number of people acquainted with my husband, though he had never spoken of them to me; and I often felt it odd and disagreeable to hear him now speak disapprovingly of some of these people who seemed to me so kind. I could not understand his coolness towards them or his endeavors to avoid many acquaintances that seemed to me flattering. Surely, the more kind people one knows, the better; and here everyone was kind.

"This is how we must manage, you see," he said to me before we left the country; "here we are little Croesueses, but in town we shall not be at all rich. So we must not stay after Easter, or go into society, or we shall get into difficulties. For your sake too I should not wish it."

"Why should we go into society?" I asked; "we shall have a look at the theaters, see our relations, go to the opera, hear some good music, and be ready to come home before Easter."

But these plans were forgotten the moment we got the Petersburg. I found myself at once in such a new and delightful world, surrounded by so many pleasures and confronted by such novel interests, that I instantly, though unconsciously, turned my back on my past life and its plans. "All that was preparatory, a mere playing at life; but here is the real thing! And there is the future too!" Such were my thoughts. The restlessness and symptoms of depression which had troubled me at home vanished at once and entirely, as if by magic. My love for my husband grew calmer, and I ceased to wonder whether he loved me less. Indeed I could not doubt his love: every thought of mine was understood at once, every feeling shared, and every wish gratified by him. His composure, if it still existed, no longer provoked me. I also began to realize that he not only loved me but was proud of me. If we paid a call, or made some new acquaintance, or gave an evening party at which I, trembling inwardly from fear of disgracing myself, acted as hostess, he often said when it was over: "Bravo, young woman! capital! you needn't be frightened; a real success!" And his praise gave me great pleasure. Soon after our arrival he wrote to his mother and asked me to add a postscript, but refused to let me see his letter; of course I insisted on reading it; and he had said: "You would not know Masha again, I don't myself. Where does she get that charming graceful self-confidence and ease, such social gifts with such simplicity and charm and kindliness? Everybody is delighted with her. I can't admire her enough myself, and should be more in love with her than ever, if that were possible."

Now I know what I am like," I thought. In my joy and pride I felt that I love him more than before. My success with all our new acquaintances was a complete surprise to me. I heard on all sides, how this uncle had taken a special fancy for me, and that aunt was raving about me; I was told by one admirer that I had no rival among the Petersburg ladies, and assured by another, a lady, that I might, if I cared, lead the fashion in society. A cousin of my husband's, in particular, a Princess D., middle-aged and very much at home in society, fell in love with me at first sight and paid me compliments which turned my head. The first time that she invited me to a ball and spoke to my husband about it, he turned to me and asked if I wished to go; I could just detect a sly smile on his face. I nodded assent and felt that I was blushing.

"She looks like a criminal when confessing what she wishes," he said with a good-natured laugh.

"But you said that we must not go into society, and you don't care for it yourself," I answered, smiling and looking imploringly at him.

"Let us go, if you want to very much," he said.

"Really, we had better not."

"Do you want to? very badly?" he asked again.

I said nothing.

"Society in itself is no great harm," he went on; "but unsatisfied social aspirations are a bad and ugly business. We must certainly accept, and we will."

"To tell you the truth," I said, "I never in my life longed for anything as much as I do for this ball."

So we went, and my delight exceeded all my expectations. It seemed to me, more than ever, that I was the center round which everything revolved, that for my sake alone this great room was lighted up and the band played, and that this crowd of people had assembled to admire me. From the hairdresser and the lady's maid to my partners and the old gentlemen promenading the ball room, all alike seemed to make it plain that they were in love with me. The general verdict formed at the ball about me and reported by my cousin, came to this: I was quite unlike the other women and had a rural simplicity and charm of my own. I was so flattered by my success that I frankly told my husband I should like to attend two or three more balls during the season, and "so get thoroughly sick of them," I added; but I did not mean what I said.

He agreed readily; and he went with me at first with obvious satisfaction. He took pleasure in my success, and seemed to have quite forgotten his former warning or to have changed his opinion.

But a time came when he was evidently bored and wearied by the life we were leading. I was too busy, however, to think about that. Even if I sometimes noticed his eyes fixed questioningly on me with a serious attentive gaze, I did not realize its meaning. I was utterly blinded by this sudden affection which I seemed to evoke in all our new acquaintances, and confused by the unfamiliar atmosphere of luxury, refinement, and novelty. It pleased me so much to find myself in these surroundings not merely his equal but his superior, and yet to love him better and more independently than before, that I could not understand what he could object to for me in society life. I had a new sense of pride and self-satisfaction when my entry at a ball attracted all eyes, while he, as if ashamed to confess his ownership of me in public, made haste to leave my side and efface himself in the crowd of black coats. "Wait a little!" I often said in my heart, when I identified his obscure and sometimes woebegone figure at the end of the room — "Wait till we get home! Then you will see and understand for whose sake I try to be beautiful and brilliant, and what it is I love in all that surrounds me this evening!" I really believed that my success pleased me only because it enabled me to give it up for his sake. One danger I recognized as possible — that I might be carried away by a fancy for some new acquaintance, and that my husband might grow jealous. But he trusted me so absolutely, and seemed so undisturbed and indifferent, and all the young men were so inferior to him, that I was not alarmed by this one danger. Yet the attention of so many people in society gave me satisfaction, flattered my vanity, and made me think that there was some merit in my love for my husband. Thus I became more offhand and self-confident in my behavior to him.

Oh, I saw you this evening carrying on a most animated conversation with Mme N.," I said one night on returning from a ball, shaking my finger at him. He had really been talking to this lady, who was a well-known figure in Petersburg society. He was more silent and depressed than usual, and I said this to rouse him up.

"What is to good of talking like that, for you especially, Masha?" he said with half-closed teeth and frowning as if in pain. "Leave that to others; it does not suit you and me. Pretence of that sort may spoil the true relation between us, which I still hope may come back."

I was ashamed and said nothing.

"Will it ever come back, Masha, do you think? he asked.

"It never was spoilt and never will be," I said; and I really believed this then.

"God grant that you are right!" he said; "if not, we ought to be going home."

But he only spoke like this once — in general he seemed as satisfied as I was, and I was so gay and so happy! I comforted myself too by thinking, "If he is bored sometimes, I endured the same thing for his sake in the country. If the relation between us has become a little different, everything will be the same again in summer, when we shall be alone in our house at Nikolskoye with Tatyana Semyonovna."

So the winter slipped by, and we stayed on, in spite of our plans, over Easter in Petersburg. A week later we were preparing to start; our packing was all done; my husband who had bought things — plants for the garden and presents for people at Nikolskoye, was in a specially cheerful and affectionate mood. Just then Princess D. came and begged us to stay till the Saturday, in order to be present at a reception to be given by Countess R. The countess was very anxious to secure me, because a foreign prince, who was visiting Petersburg and had seen me already at a ball, wished to make my acquaintance; indeed this was his motive for attending the reception, and he declared that I was the most beautiful woman in Russia. All the world was to be there; and, in a word, it would really be too bad, if I did not go too.

My husband was talking to someone at the other end of the drawing room.

"So you will go, won't you, Mary?" said the Princess.

"We meant to start for the country the day after tomorrow," I answered undecidedly, glancing at my husband. Our eyes met, and he turned away at once.

"I must persuade him to stay," she said, "and then we can go on Saturday and turn all heads. All right?"

"It would upset our plans; and we have packed," I answered, beginning to give way.

"She had better go this evening and make her curtsey to the Prince," my husband called out from the other end of the room; and he spoke in a tone of suppressed irritation which I had never heard from him before.

"I declare he's jealous, for the first time in his life," said the lady, laughing. "But it's not for the sake of the Prince I urge it, Sergey Mikhaylych, but for all our sakes. The Countess was so anxious to have her."

"It rests with her entirely," my husband said coldly, and then left the room.

I saw that he was much disturbed, and this pained me. I gave no positive promise. As soon as our visitor left, I went to my husband. He was walking up and down his room, thinking, and neither saw nor heard me when I came in on tiptoe.

Looking at him, I said to myself: "He is dreaming already of his dear Nikolskoye, our morning coffee in the bright drawing room, the land and the laborers, our evenings in the music room, and our secret midnight suppers." Then I decided in my own heart: "Not for all the balls and all the flattering princes in the world will I give up his glad confusion and tender cares." I was just about to say that I did not wish to go to the ball and would refuse, when he looked round, saw me, and frowned. His face, which had been gentle and thoughtful, changed at once to its old expression of sagacity, penetration, and patronizing composure. He would not show himself to me as a mere man, but had to be a demigod on a pedestal.

"Well, my dear?" he asked, turning towards me with an unconcerned air.

I said nothing. I ws provoked, because he was hiding his real self from me, and would not continue to be the man I loved.

"Do you want to go to this reception on Saturday?" he asked.

"I did, but you disapprove. Besides, our things are all packed," I said.

Never before had I heard such coldness in his tone to me, and never before seen such coldness in his eye.

"I shall order the things to be unpacked," he said, "and I shall stay till Tuesday. So you can go to the party, if you like. I hope you will; but I shall not go."

Without looking at me, he began to walk about the room jerkily, as his habit was when perturbed.

"I simply can't understand you," I said, following him with my eyes from where I stood. "You say that you never lose self-control" (he had never really said so); "then why do you talk to me so strangely? I am ready on your account to sacrifice this pleasure, and then you, in a sarcastic tone which is new from you to me, insist that I should go."

"So you make a sacrifice!" he threw special emphasis on the last word. "Well, so do I. What could be better? We compete in generosity — what an example of family happiness!"

Such harsh and contemptuous language I had never heard from his lips before. I was not abashed, but mortified by his contempt; and his harshness did not frighten me but made me harsh too. How could he speak thus, he who was always so frank and simple and dreaded insincerity in our speech to one another? And what had I done that he should speak so? I really intended to sacrifice for his sake a pleasure in which I could see no harm; and a moment ago I loved him and understood his feelings as well as ever. We had changed parts: now he avoided direct and plain words, and I desired them.

"You are much changed," I said, with a sigh. "How am I guilty before you? It is not this party — you have something else, some old count against me. Why this insincerity? You used to be so afraid of it yourself. Tell me plainly what you complain of." "What will he say?" thought I, and reflected with some complacency that I had done nothing all winter which he could find fault with.

I went into the middle of the room, so that he had to pass close to me, and looked at him. I thought, "He will come and clasp me in his arms, and there will be an end of it." I was even sorry that I should not have the chance of proving him wrong. But he stopped at the far end of the room and looked at me.

"Do you not understand yet?" he asked.

"No, I don't."

"Then I must explain. what I feel, and cannot help feeling, positively sickens me for the first time in my life." He stopped, evidently startled by the harsh sound of his own voice.

"What do you mean?" I asked, with tears of indignation in my eyes.

"It sickens me that the Prince admired you, and you therefore run to meet him, forgetting your husband and yourself and womanly dignity; and you wilfully misunderstand what your want of self-respect makes your husband feel for you: you actually come to your husband and speak of the "sacrifice" you are making, by which you mean — "To show myself to His Highness is a great pleasure to me, but I sacrifice' it."

The longer he spoke, the more he was excited by the sound of his own voice, which was hard and rough and cruel. I had never seen him, had never thought of seeing him, like that. The blood rushed to my heart and I was frightened; but I felt that I had nothing to be ashamed of, and the excitement of wounded vanity made me eager to punish him.

"I have long been expecting this," I said. "Go on. Go on!"

"What you expected, I don't know," he went on; "but I might well expect the worst, when I saw you day after day sharing the dirtiness and idleness and luxury of this foolish society, and it has come at last. Never have I felt such shame and pain as now — pain for myself, when your friend thrusts her unclean fingers into my heart and speaks of my jealousy! — jealousy of a man whom neither you nor I know; and you refuse to understand me and offer to make a sacrifice for me — and what sacrifice? I am ashamed for you, for your degradation! . . .Sacrifice!" he repeated again.

"Ah, so this is a husband's power," thought I: "to insult and humiliate a perfectly innocent woman. Such may be a husband's rights, but I will not submit to them." I felt the blood leave my face and a strange distension of my nostrils, as I said, "No! I make no sacrifice on your account. I shall go to the party on Saturday without fail."

"And I hope you may enjoy it. But all is over between us two!" he cried out in a fit of unrestrained fury. "But you shall not torture me any longer! I was a fool, when I . . .", but his lips quivered, and he refrained with a visible effort from ending the sentence.

I feared and hated him at that moment. I wished to say a great deal to him and punish him for all his insults; but if I had opened my mouth, I should have lost my dignity by bursting into tears. I said nothing and left the room. But as soon as I ceased to hear his footsteps, I was horrified at what we had done. I feared that the tie which had made all my happiness might really be snapped forever; and I thought of going back. But then I wondered: "Is he calm enough now to understand me, if I mutely stretch out my hand and look at him? Will he realize my generosity? What if he calls my grief a mere pretence? Or he may feel sure that he is right and accept my repentance and forgive me with unruffled pride. And why, oh why, did he whom I loved so well insult me so cruelly?"

I went not to him but to my own room, where I sat for a long time and cried. I recalled with horror each word of our conversation, and substituted different words, kind words, for those that we had spoken, and added others; and then again I remembered the reality with horror and a feeling of injury. In the evening I went down for tea and met my husband in the presence of a friend who was staying with us; and it seemed to me that a wide gulf had opened between us from that day. Our friend asked me when we were to start; and before I could speak, my husband answered:

"On Tuesday," he said; "we have to stay for Countess R.'s reception." He turned to me: "I believe you intend to go?" he asked.

His matter-of-fact tone frightened me, and I looked at him timidly. His eyes were directed straight at me with an unkind and scornful expression; his voice was cold and even.

"Yes," I answered.

When we were alone that evening, he came up to me and held out his hand.

"Please forget what I said to you today," he began.

As I took his hand, a smile quivered on my lips and the tears were ready to flow; but he took his hand away and sat down on an armchair at some distance, as if fearing a sentimental scene. "Is it possible that he still thinks himself in the right?" I wondered; and, though I was quite ready to explain and to beg that we might not go to the party, the words died on my lips.

"I must write to my mother that we have put off our departure," he said; "otherwise she will be uneasy."

"When do you think of going?" I asked.

"On Tuesday, after the reception," he replied.

"I hope it is not on my account," I said, looking into his eyes; but those eyes merely looked — they said nothing, and a veil seemed to cover them from me. His face seemed to me to have grown suddenly old and disagreeable.

We went to the reception, and good friendly relations between us seemed to have been restored, but these relations were quite different from what they had been.

At the party I was sitting with other ladies when the Prince came up to me, so that I had to stand up in order to speak to him. As I rose, my eyes involuntarily sought my husband. He was looking at me from the other end of the room, and now turned away. I was seized by a sudden sense of shame and pain; in my confusion I blushed all over my face and neck under the Prince's eye. But I was forced to stand and listen, while he spoke, eyeing me from his superior height. Our conversation was soon over: there was no room for him beside me, and he, no doubt, felt that I was uncomfortable with him. We talked of the last ball, of where I should spend the summer, and so on. As he left me, he expressed a wish to make the acquaintance of my husband, and I saw them meet and begin a conversation at the far end of the room. The Prince evidently said something about me; for he smiled in the middle of their talk and looked in my direction.

My husband suddenly flushed up. He made a low bow and turned away from the prince without being dismissed. I blushed too: I was ashamed of the impression which I and, still more, my husband must have made on the Prince. Everyone, I thought, must have noticed my awkward shyness when I was presented, and my husband's eccentric behavior. "Heaven knows how they will interpret such conduct? Perhaps they know already about my scene with my husband!"

Princess D. drove me home, and on the way I spoke to her about my husband. My patience was at an end, and I told her the whole story of what had taken place between us owing to this unlucky party. To calm me, she said that such differences were very common and quite unimportant, and that our quarrel would leave no trace behind. She explained to me her view of my husband's character — that he had become very stiff and unsociable. I agreed, and believed that I had learned to judge him myself more calmly and more truly.

but when I was alone with my husband later, the thought that I had sat in judgment upon him weighed like a crime upon my conscience; and I felt that the gulf which divided us had grown still greater.

CHAPTER 3

From that day there was a complete change in our life and our relations to each other. We were no longer as happy when we were alone together as before. To certain subjects we gave a wide berth, and conversation flowed more easily in the presence of a third person. When the talk turned on life in the country, or on a ball, we were uneasy and shrank from looking at one another. Both of us knew where the gulf between us lay, and seemed afraid to approach it. I was convinced that he was proud and irascible, and that I must be careful not to touch him on his weak point. He was equally sure that I disliked the country and was dying for social distraction, and that he must put up with this unfortunate taste of mine. We both avoided frank conversation on these topics, and each misjudged the other. We had long ceased to think each other the most perfect people in the world; each now judged the other in secret, and measured the offender by the standard of other people. I fell ill before we left Petersburg, and we went from there to a house near town, from which my husband went on alone, to join his mother at Nikolskoye. By that time I was well enough to have gone with him, but he urged me to stay on the pretext of my health. I knew, however, that he was really afraid we should be uncomfortable together in the country; so I did not insist much, and he went off alone. I felt it dull and solitary in his absence; but when he came back, I saw that he did not add to my life what he had added formerly. In the old days every thought and experience weighed on me like a crime till I had imparted it to him; every action and word of his seemed to me a model of perfection; we often laughed for joy at the mere sight of each other. But these relations had changed, so imperceptibly that we had not even noticed their disappearance. Separate interests and cares, which we no longer tried to share, made their appearance, and even the fact of our estrangement ceased to trouble us. The idea became familiar, and, before a year had passed, each could look at the other without confusion. His fits of boyish merriment with me had quite vanished; his mood of calm indulgence to all that passed, which used to provoke me, had disappeared; there was an end of those penetrating looks which used to confuse and delight me, an end of the ecstasies and prayers which we once shared in common. We did not even meet often: he was continually absent, with no fears or regrets for leaving me alone; and I was constantly in society, where I did not need him.

There were no further scenes or quarrels between us. I tried to satisfy him, he carried out all my wishes, and we seemed to love each other.

When we were by ourselves, which we seldom were, I felt neither joy nor excitement nor embarrassment in his company: it seemed like being alone. I realized that he was my husband and no mere stranger, a good man, and as familiar to me as my own self. I was convinced that I knew just what he would say and do, and how he would look; and if anything he did surprised me, I concluded that he had made a mistake. I expected nothing from him. In a word, he was my husband — and that was all. It seemed to me that things must be so, as a matter of course, and that no other relations between us had ever existed. When he left home, especially at first, I was lonely and frightened and felt keenly my need of support; when he came back, I ran to his arms with joy, though tow hours later my joy was quite forgotten, and I found nothing to say to him. Only at moments which sometimes occurred between us of quiet undemonstrative affection, I felt something wrong and some pain at my heart, and I seemed to read the same story in his eyes. I was conscious of a limit to tenderness, which he seemingly would not, and I could not, overstep. This saddened me sometimes; but I had no leisure to reflect on anything, and my regret for a change which I vaguely realized I tried to drown in the distractions which were always within my reach. Fashionable life, which had dazzled me at first by its glitter and flattery of my self-love, now took entire command of my nature, became a habit, laid its fetters upon me, and monopolized my capacity for feeling. I could not bear solitude, and was afraid to reflect on my position. My whole day, from late in the morning till late at night, was taken up by the claims of society; even if I stayed at home, my time was not my own. this no longer seemed to me either gay or dull, but it seemed that so, and not otherwise, it always had to be.

So three years passed, during which our relations to one another remained unchanged and seemed to have taken a fixed shape which could not become either better or worse. Though two events of importance in our family life took place during that time, neither of them changed my own life. These were the birth of my first child and the death of Tatyana Semyonovna. At first the feeling of motherhood did take hold of me with such power, and produce in me such a passion of unanticipated joy, that I believed this would prove the beginning of a new life for me. But, in the course of two months, when I began to go out again, my feeling grew weaker and weaker, till it passed into mere habit and the lifeless performance of a duty. My husband, on the contrary, from the birth of our first boy, became his old self again — gentle, composed, and home-loving, and transferred to the child his old tenderness and gaiety. Many a night when I went, dressed for a ball, to the nursery, to sign the child with the cross before he slept, I found my husband there and felt his eyes fixed on me with something of reproof in their serious gaze. Then I was ashamed and even shocked by my own callousness, and asked myself if I was worse than other women. "But it can't be helped," I said to myself; "I love my child, but to sit beside him all day long would bore me; and nothing will make me pretend what I do not really feel."

His mother's death was a great sorrow to my husband; he said that he found it painful to go on living at Nikolskoye. For myself, although I mourned for her and sympathized with my husband's sorrow, Yet I found life in that house easier and pleasanter after her death. Most of those three years we spent in town: I went only once to Nikolskoye for two months; and the third year we went abroad and spent the summer at Baden.

I was then twenty-one; our financial position was, I believed, satisfactory; my domestic life gave me all that I asked of it; everyone I knew, it seemed to me, loved me; my health was good; I was the best-dressed woman in Baden; I knew that I was good looking; the weather was fine; I enjoyed the atmosphere of beauty and refinement; and, in short, I was in excellent spirits. They had once been even higher at Nikolskoye, when my happiness was in myself and came from the feeling that I deserved to be happy, and from the anticipation of still greater happiness to come. That was a different state of things; but I did very well this summer also. I had no special wishes or hopes of fears; it seemed to me that my life was full and my conscience easy. Among all the visitors at Baden that season there was no one man whom I preferred to the rest, or even to our old ambassador, Prince K., who was assiduous in his attentions to me. One was young, and another old; one was English and fair, another French and wore a beard — to me they were all alike, but all indispensable. Indistinguishable as they were, they together made up the atmosphere which I found so pleasant. But there was one, an Italian marquis, who stood out from the rest by reason of the boldness with which he expressed his admiration. He seized every opportunity of being with me — danced with me, rode with me, and met me at the casino; and everywhere he spoke to me of my charms. Several times I saw him from my windows loitering round our hotel, and the fixed gaze of his bright eyes often troubled me, and made me blush and turn away. He was young, handsome, and well-mannered; and above all, by his smile and the expression of his brow, he resembled my husband, though much handsomer than he. He struck me by this likeness, though in general, in his lips, eyes, and long chin, there was something coarse and animal which contrasted with my husband's charming expression of kindness and noble serenity. I supposed him to be passionately in love with me, and thought of him sometimes with proud commiseration. When I tried at times to soothe him and change his tone to one of easy, half-friendly confidence, he resented the suggestion with vehemence, and continued to disquiet me by a smoldering passion which was ready at any moment to burst forth. Though I would not own it even to myself, I feared him and often thought of him against my sill. My husband knew him, and greeted him — even more than other acquaintances of ours who regarded him only as my husband — with coldness and disdain.

Towards the end of the season I fell ill and stayed indoors for a fortnight. The first evening that I went out again to hear the band, I learnt that Lady S., an Englishwoman famous for her beauty, who had long been expected, had arrived in my absence. My return was welcomed, and a group gathered round me; but a more distinguished group attended the beautiful stranger. She and her beauty were the one subject of conversation around me. When I saw her, she was really beautiful, but her self-satisfied expression struck me as disagreeable, and I said so. That day everything that had formerly seemed amusing, seemed dull. Lady S. arranged an expedition to ruined castle for the next day; but I declined to be of the party. Almost everyone else went; and my opinion of Baden underwent a complete change. Everything and everybody seemed to me stupid and tiresome; I wanted to cry, to break off my cure, to return to Russia. There was some evil feeling in my soul, but I did not yet acknowledge it to myself. Pretending that I was not strong, I ceased to appear at crowded parties; if I went out, it was only in the morning by myself, to drink the waters; and my only companion was Mme M., a Russian lady, with whom I sometimes took drives in the surrounding country. My husband was absent: he had gone to Heidelberg for a time, intending to return to Russia when my cure was over, and only paid me occasional visits at Baden.

One day when Lady S. had carried off all the company on a hunting expedition, Mme M. and I drove in the afternoon to the castle. While our carriage moved slowly along the winding road, bordered by ancient chestnut-trees and commanding a vista of the pretty and pleasant country round Baden, with the setting sun lighting it up, our conversation took a more serious turn than had ever happened to us before. I had known my companion for a long time; but she appeared to me now in a new light, as a well-principled and intelligent woman, to whom it was possible to speak without reserve, and whose friendship was worth having. We spoke of our private concerns, of our children, of the emptiness of life at Baden, till we felt a longing for Russia and the Russian countryside. When we entered the castle we were still under the impression of this serious feeling. Within the walls there was shade and coolness; the sunlight played from above upon the ruins. Steps and voices were audible. The landscape, charming enough but cold to a Russian eye, lay before us in the frame made by a doorway. We sat down to rest and watched the sunset in silence. The voices now sounded louder, and I thought I heard my own name. I listened and could not help overhearing every word. I recognized the voices: the speakers were the Italian marquis and a French friend of his whom I knew also. They were talking of me and of Lady S., and the Frenchman was comparing us as rival beauties. Though he said nothing insulting, his words made my pulse quicken. He explained in detail the good points of us both. I was already a mother, while Lady S. was only nineteen; though I had the advantage in hair, my rival had a better figure. "Besides," he added, "Lady S. is a real grande dame, and the other is nothing in particular, only one of those obscure Russian princesses who turn up here nowadays in such numbers." He ended by saying that I was wise in not attempting to compete with Lady S., and that I was completely buried as far as Baden was concerned.

"I am sorry for her — unless indeed she takes a fancy to console herself with you," he added with a hard ringing laugh.

"If she goes away, I follow her" — the words were blurted out in an Italian accent.

"Happy man! he is still capable of a passion!" laughed the Frenchman.

"Passion!" said the other voice and then was still for a moment. "It is a necessity to me: I cannot live without it. To make life a romance is the one thing worth doing. And with me romance never breaks off in the middle, and this affair I shall carry through to the end."

"Bonne chance, mon ami!" said the Frenchman.

They now turned a corner, and the voices stopped. Then we heard them coming down the steps, and a few minutes later they came out upon us by a side door. They were much surprised to see us.

I blushed when the marquis approached me, and felt afraid when we left the castle and he offered me his arm. I could not refuse, and we set off for the carriage, walking behind Mme M. and his friend. I was mortified by what the Frenchman had said of me, though I secretly admitted that he had only put in words what I felt myself; but the plain speaking of the Italian had surprised and upset me by its coarseness. I was tormented by the thought that, though I had overheard him, he showed no fear of me. It was hateful to have him so close to me; and I walked fast after the other couple, not looking at him or answering him and trying to hold his arm in such a way as not to hear him. He spoke of the fine view, of the unexpected pleasure of our meeting, and so on; but I was not listening. My thoughts were with my husband, my child, my country; I felt ashamed distressed, anxious; I was in a hurry to get back to my solitary room in the Hotel de Bade, there to think at leisure of the storm of feeling that had just risen in my heart. But Mme M. walked slowly, it was still a long way to the carriage, and my escort seemed to loiter on purpose as if he wished to detain me. "None of that!" I thought, and resolutely quickened my pace. But it soon became unmistakable that he was detaining me and even pressing my arm. Mme M. turned a corner, and we were quite alone. I was afraid.

"Excuse me," I said coldly and tried to free my arm; but the lace of my sleeve caught on a button of his coat. Bending towards me, he began to unfasten it, and his ungloved fingers touched my arm. A feeling new to me, half horror and half pleasure, sent an icy shiver down my back. I looked at him, intending by my coldness to convey all the contempt I felt for him; but my look expressed nothing but fear and excitement. His liquid blazing eyes, right up against my face, stared strangely at me, at my neck and breast; both his hands fingered my arm above the wrist; his parted lips were saying that he loved me, and that I was all the world to him; and those lips were coming nearer and nearer, and those hands were squeezing mine harder and harder and burning me. A fever ran through my veins, my sight grew dim, I trembled, and the words intended to check him died in my throat. Suddenly I felt a kiss on my cheek. Trembling all over and turning cold, I stood still and stared at him. Unable to speak or move, I stood there, horrified, expectant, even desirous. It was over in a moment, but the moment was horrible! In that short time I saw him exactly as he was — the low straight forehead (that forehead so like my husband's!) under the straw hat; the handsome regular nose and dilated nostrils; the long waxed mustache and short beard; the close-shaved cheeks and sunburned neck. I hated and feared him; he was utterly repugnant and alien to me. And yet the excitement and passion of this hateful strange man raised a powerful echo in my own heart; I felt an irresistible longing to surrender myself to the kisses of that coarse handsome mouth, and to the pressure of those white hands with their delicate veins and jewelled fingers; I was tempted to throw myself headlong into the abyss of forbidden delights that had suddenly opened up before me.

"I am so unhappy already," I thought; "let more and more storms of unhappiness burst over my head!"

He put one arm round me and bent towards my face. "Better so!" I thought: "let sin and shame cover me ever deeper and deeper!"

"Je vous aime!" he whispered in the voice which was so like my husband's. At once I thought of my husband and child, as creatures once precious to me who had now passed altogether out of my life. At that moment I heard Mme M.'s voice; she called to me from round the corner. I came to myself, tore my hand away without looking at him, and almost ran after her: I only looked at him after she and I were already seated in the carriage. Then I saw him raise his hat and ask some commonplace question with a smile. He little knew the inexpressible aversion I felt for him at that moment.

My life seemed so wretched, the future so hopeless, the past so black! When Mme M. spoke, her words meant nothing to me. I thought that she talked only our of pity, and to hide the contempt I aroused in her. In every word and every look I seemed to detect this contempt and insulting pity. The shame of that kiss burned my cheek, and the thought of my husband and child was more than I could bear. When I was alone in my own room, I tried to think over my position; but I was afraid to be alone. Without drinking the tea which was brought me, and uncertain of my own motives, I got ready with feverish haste to catch the evening train and join my husband at Heidelberg.

I found seats for myself and my maid in an empty carriage. When the train started and the fresh air blew through the window on my face, I grew more composed and pictured my past and future to myself more clearly. The course of our married life from the time of our first visit to Petersburg now presented itself to me in a new light, and lay like a reproach on my conscience. For the first time I clearly recalled our start at Nikolskoye and our plans for the future; and for the first time I asked myself what happiness had my husband had since then. I felt that I had behaved badly to him. "By why", I asked myself, "did he not stope me? Why did he make pretences? Why did he always avoid explanations? Why did he insult me? Why did he not use the power of his love to influence me? Or did he not love me?" But whether he was to blame or not, I still felt the kiss of that strange man upon my cheek. The nearer we got to Heidelberg, the clearer grew my picture of my husband, and the more I dreaded our meeting. "I shall tell him all," I thought, "and wipe out everything with tears of repentance; and he will forgive me." But I did not know myself what I meant by "everything"; and I did not believe in my heart that he would forgive me.

As soon as I entered my husband's room and saw his calm though surprised expression, I felt at once that I had nothing to tell him, no confession to make, and nothing to ask forgiveness for. I had to suppress my unspoken grief and penitence.

"What put this into your head?" he asked. "I meant to go to Baden tomorrow." Then he looked more closely at me and seemed to take alarm. "What's the matter with you? What has happened?" he said.

"Nothing at all," I replied, almost breaking down. "I am not going back.

Let us go home, tomorrow if you like, to Russia."

For some time he said nothing but looked at me attentively. Then he said, "But do tell me what has happened to you."

I blushed involuntarily and looked down. There came into his eyes a flash of anger and displeasure. Afraid of what he might imagine, I said with a power of pretence that surprised myself:

"Nothing at all has happened. It was merely that I grew weary and sad by myself; and I have been thinking a great deal of our way of life and of you. I have long been to blame towards you. Why do you take me abroad, when you can't bear it yourself? I have long been to blame. Let us go back to Nikolskoye and settle there for ever."

"Spare us these sentimental scenes, my dear," he said coldly. "To go back to Nikolskoye is a good idea, for our money is running short; but the notion of stopping there for ever' is fanciful. I know you would not settle down. Have some tea, and you will feel better," and he rose to ring for the waiter.

I imagined all he might be thinking about me; and I was offended by the horrible thoughts which I ascribed to him when I encountered the dubious and shame-faced look he directed at me. "He will not and cannot understand me." I said I would go and look at the child, and I left the room. I wished to be alone, and to cry and cry and cry . . .

CHAPTER 4

The house at Nikolskoye, so long unheated and uninhabited, came to life again; but much of the past was dead beyond recall. Tatyana Semyonovna was no more, and we were now alone together. But far from desiring such close companionship, we even found it irksome. To me that winter was the more trying because I was in bad health, from which In only recovered after the birth of my second son. My husband and I were still on the same terms as during our life in Petersburg: we were coldly friendly to each other; but in the country each room and wall and sofa recalled what he had once been to me, and what I had lost. It was if some unforgiven grievance held us apart, as if he were punishing me and pretending not to be aware of it. But there was nothing to ask pardon for, no penalty to deprecate; my punishment was merely this, that he did not give his whole heart and mind to me as he used to do; but he did not give it to anyone or to anything; as though he had no longer a heart to give. Sometimes it occurred to me that he was only pretending to be like that, in order to hurt me, and that the old feeling was still alive in his breast; and I tried to call it forth. But I always failed: he always seemed to avoid frankness, evidently suspecting me of insincerity, and dreading the folly of any emotional display. I could read in his face and the tone of his voice, "What is the good of talking? I know all the facts already, and I know what is on the tip of your tongue, and I know that you will say one thing and do another." At first I was mortified by his dread of frankness, but I came later to think that it was rather the absence, on his part, of any need of frankness. It would never have occurred to me now, to tell him of a sudden that I loved him, or to ask him to repeat the prayers with me or listen while Ii played the piano. Our intercourse came to be regulated by a fixed code of good manners. We lived our separate lives: he had his own occupations in which I was not needed, and which I no longer wished to share, while I continued my idle life which no longer vexed or grieved him. The children were still too young to form a bond between us.

But spring came round and brought Katya and Sonya to spend the summer with us in the country. as the house at Nikolskoye was under repair, we went to live at my old home at Pokrovskoye. The old house was unchanged — the veranda, the folding table and the piano in the sunny drawing room, and my old bedroom with its white curtains and the dreams of my girlhood which I seemed to have left behind me there. In that room there were two beds: one had been mine, and in it now my plump little Kokosha lay sprawling, when I went at night to sign him with the cross; the other was a crib, in which the little face of my baby, Vanya, peeped out from his swaddling clothes. Often when I had made the sign over them and remained standing in the middle of the quiet room, suddenly there rose up from all the corners, from the walls and curtains, old forgotten visions of youth. Old voices began to sing the songs of my girlhood. Where were those visions now? where were those dear old sweet songs? All that I had hardly dared to hope for had come to pass. My vague confused dreams had become a reality, and the reality had become an oppressive, difficult, and joyless life. All remained the same — the garden visible through the window, the grass, the path, the very same bench over there above the dell, the same song of the nightingale by the pond, the same lilacs in full bloom, the same moon shining above the house; and yet, in everything such a terrible inconceivable change! Such coldness in all that might have been near and dear! Just as in old times Katya and I sit quietly alone together in the parlour and talk, and talk of him. But Katya has grown wrinkled and pale; and her eyes no longer shine with joy and hope, but express only sympathy, sorrow, and regret. We do not go into raptures as we used to, we judge him coolly; we do not wonder what we have done to deserve such happiness, or long to proclaim our thoughts to all the world. No! we whisper together like conspirators and ask each other for the hundredth time why all has changed so sadly. Yet he was still the same man, save for the deeper furrow between his eyebrows and the whiter hair on his temples; but his serious attentive look was constantly veiled from me by a cloud. And I am the same woman, but without love or desire for love, with no longing for work and not content with myself. My religious ecstasies, my love for my husband, the fullness of my former life — all these now seem utterly remote and visionary. Once it seemed so plain and right that to live for others was happiness; but now it has become unintelligible. Why live for others, when life had no attraction even for oneself?

I had given up my music altogether since the time of our first visit to Petersburg; but now the old piano and the old music tempted me to begin again.

One day i was not well and stayed indoors alone. My husband had taken Katya and Sonya to see the new buildings at Nikolskoye. Tea was laid; I went downstairs and while waiting for them sat down at the piano. I opened the "Moonlight sonata" and began to play. There was no one within sight or sound, the windows were open over the garden, and the familiar sounds floated through the room with a solemn sadness. At the end of the first movement I looked round instinctively to the corner where he used once to sit and listen to my playing. He was not there; his chair, long unmoved, was still in its place; through the window I could see a lilac bush against the light of the setting sun; the freshness of evening streamed in through the open windows. I rested my elbows on the piano and covered my face with both hands; and so I sat for a long time, thinking. I recalled with pain the irrevocable past, and timidly imagined the future. But for me there seemed to be no future, no desires at all and no hopes. "Can life be over for me?" I thought with horror; then I looked up, and, trying to forget and not to think, I began playing the same movement over again. "Oh, God!" I prayed, "forgive me if I have sinned, or restore to me all that once blossomed in my heart, or teach me what to do and how to live now." There was a sound of wheels on the grass and before the steps of the house; then I heard cautious and familiar footsteps pass along the veranda and cease; but my heart no longer replied to the sound. When I stopped playing the footsteps were behind me and a hand was laid on my shoulder.

"How clever of you to think of playing that!" he said.

I said nothing.

"Have you had tea?" he asked.

I shook my head without looking at him — I was unwilling to let him see the signs of emotion on my face.

"They'll be here immediately," he said; "the horse gave trouble, and they got out on the high road to walk home."

"Let us wait for them," I said, and went out to the veranda, hoping that he would follow; but he asked about the children and went upstairs to see them. Once more his presence and simple kindly voice made me doubt if I had really lost anything. What more could I wish? "He is kind and gentle, a good husband, a good father; I don't know myself what more I want." I sat down under the veranda awning on the very bench on which I had sat when we became engaged. The sun had set, it was growing dark, and a little spring rain cloud hung over the house and garden, and only behind the trees the horizon was clear, with the fading glow of twilight, in which one star had just begun to twinkle. The landscape, covered by the shadow of the cloud, seemed waiting for the light spring shower. There was not a breath of wind; not a single leaf or blade of grass stirred; the scent of lilac and bird cherry was so strong in the garden and veranda that it seemed as if all the air was in flower; it came in wafts, now stronger and now weaker, till one longed to shut both eyes and hears and drink in that fragrance only. The dahlias and rose bushes, not yet in flower, stood motionless on the black mould of the border, looking as if they were growing slowly upwards on their white-shaved props; beyond the dell, the frogs were making the most of their time before the rain drove them to the pond, croaking busily and loudly. Only the high continuous note of water falling at some distance rose above their croaking. From time to time the nightingales called to one another, and I could hear them flitting restlessly from bush to bush. Again this spring a nightingale had tried to build in a bush under the window, and I heard her fly off across the avenue when I went into the veranda. From there she whistled once and then stopped; she, too, was expecting the rain.

I tried in vain to calm my feelings: I had a sense of anticipation and regret.

He came downstairs again and sat down beside me.

"I am afraid they will get wet," he said.

"Yes," I answered; and we sat for long without speaking.

The cloud came down lower and lower with no wind. The air grew stiller and more fragrant. Suddenly a drop fell on the canvas awning and seemed to rebound from it; then another broke on the gravel path; soon there was a splash on the burdock leaves, and a fresh shower of big drops came down faster and faster. Nightingales and frogs were both dumb; only the high note of the falling water, though the rain made it seem more distant, still went on; and a bird, which must have sheltered among the dry leaves near the veranda, steadily repeated its two unvarying notes. My husband got up to go in.

"Where are you going?" I asked, trying to keep him; "it is so pleasant here."

"We must send them an umbrella and galoshes," he replied.

"Don't trouble — it will soon be over."

He thought I was right, and we remained together in the veranda. I rested one hand upon the wet slippery rail and put my head out. The fresh rain wetted my hair and neck in places. The cloud, growing lighter and thinner, was passing overhead; the steady patter of the rain gave place to occasional drops that fell from the sky or dripped from the trees. The frogs began to croak again in the dell; the nightingales woke up and began to call from the dripping bushes from one side and then from another. The whole prospect before us grew clear.

"How delightful!" he said, seating himself on the veranda rail and passing a hand over my wet hair.

This simple caress had on me the effect of a reproach: I felt inclined to cry.

"What more can a man need?" he said; "I am so content now that I want nothing; I am perfectly happy!"

He told me a different story once, I thought. He had said that, however great his happiness might be, he always wanted more and more. Now he is calm and contented; while my heart is full of unspoken repentance and unshed tears.

"I think it delightful too," I said; "but I am sad just because of the beauty of it all. All is so fair and lovely outside me, while my own heart is confused and baffled and full of vague unsatisfied longing. Is it possible that there is no element of pain, no yearning for the past, in your enjoyment of nature?"

He took his hand off my head and was silent for a little.

"I used to feel that too," he said, as though recalling it, "especially in spring. I used to sit up all night too, with my hopes and fears for company, and good company they were! But life was all before me then. Now it is all behind me, and I am content with what I have. I find life capital," he added with such careless confidence, that I believed, whatever pain it gave me to hear it, that it was the truth.

"But is there nothing you wish for?" I asked.

"I don't ask for impossibilities," he said, guessing my thoughts. "You go and get your head wet," he added, stroking my head like a child's and again passing his hand over the wet hair; "you envy the leaves and the grass their wetting from the rain, and you would like yourself to be the grass and the leaves and the rain. But I am contented to enjoy them and everything else that is good and young and happy."

"And do you regret nothing of the past?" I asked, while my heart grew heavier and heavier.

Again he thought for a time before replying. I saw that he wished to reply with perfect frankness.

"Nothing," he said shortly.

"Not true! not true!" I said, turning towards him and looking into his eyes. "Do you really not regret the past?"

"No!" he repeated; "I am grateful for it, but I don't regret it."

"But would you not like to have it back?" I asked.

"No; I might as well wish to have wings. It is impossible."

"And would you not alter the past? do you not reproach yourself or me?"

"No, never! It was all for the best."

"Listen to me!" I said touching his arm to make him look round. "Why did you never tell me that you wished me to live as you really wished me to? Why did you give me a freedom for which I was unfit? Why did you stop teaching me? If you had wished it, if you had guided me differently, none of all this would have happened!" said I in a voice that increasingly expressed cold displeasure and reproach in place of the love of former days.

"What would not have happened?" he asked, turning to me in surprise. "As it is, there is nothing wrong. things are all right, quite all right," he added with a smile.

"does he really not understand?" I thought; "or still worse, does he not wish to understand?"

Then I suddenly broke out. "Had you acted differently, I should not now be punished, for no fault at all, by your indifference and even contempt, and you would not have taken from me unjustly all that I valued in life!"

"What do you mean, my dear one?" he asked — he seemed not to understand me.

"No! don't interrupt me! You have taken from me your confidence, your love, even your respect; for I cannot believe, when I think of the past, that you still love me. No! don't speak! I must once for all say out what has long been torturing me. Is it my fault that I knew nothing of life, and that you left me to learn experience for myself? Is it my fault that now, when I have gained the knowledge and have been struggling for nearly a year to come back to you, you push me away and pretend not to understand what I want? And you always do it so that it is impossible to reproach you, while I am guilty and unhappy. Yes, you wish to drive me out again to that life which might rob us both of happiness."

"How did I show that!" he asked in evident alarm and surprise.

"No later than yesterday you said, and you constantly say, that I can never settle down here, and that we must spend this winter too at Petersburg; and I hate Petersburg!" I went on, "Instead of supporting me, you avoid all plain speaking, you never say a single frank affectionate word to me. And then, when I fall utterly, you will reproach me and rejoice in my fall."

"Stop!" he said with cold severity. "You have no right to say that. It only proves that you are ill-disposed towards me, that you don't . . ."

"That I don't love you? Don't hesitate to say it!" I cried, and the tears began to flow. I sat down on the bench and covered my face with my handkerchief.

"So that is how he understood me!" I thought, trying to restrain the sobs which choked me. "gone, gone is our former love!" said a voice at my heart. He did not come close or try to comfort me. He was hurt by what I had said. When he spoke, his tone was cool and dry.

"I don't know what you reproach me with," he began. "If you mean that I don't love you as I once did . . ."

"Did love!" I said, with my face buried in the handkerchief, while the bitter tears fell still more abundantly.

"If so, time is to blame for that, and we ourselves. Each time of life has its own kind of love." He was silent for a moment. "Shall I tell you the whole truth, if you really wish for frankness? In that summer when I first knew you, I used to lie awake all night, thinking about you, and I made that love myself, and it grew and grew in my heart. So again, in Petersburg and abroad, in the course of horrible sleepless nights, I strove to shatter and destroy that love, which had come to torture me. I did not destroy it, but I destroyed that part of it which gave me pain. Then I grew calm; and I feel love still, but it is a different kind of love."

"You call it love, but I call it torture!" I said. "Why did you allow me to go into society, if you thought so badly of it that you ceased to love me on that account?"

"No, it was not society, my dear," he said.

"Why did you not exercise your authority?" I went on: "why did you not lock me up or kill me? That would have been better than the loss of all that formed my happiness. I should have been happy, instead of being ashamed."

I began to sob again and hid my face.

Just then Katya and Sonya, wet and cheerful, came out to the veranda, laughing and talking loudly. They were silent as soon as they saw us, and went in again immediately.

We remained silent for a long time. I had had my cry out and felt relieved. I glanced at him. He was sitting with his head resting on his hand; he intended to make some reply to my glance, but only sighed deeply and resumed his former position.

I went up to him and removed his hand. His eyes turned thoughtfully to my face.

"Yes," he began, as if continuing his thoughts aloud, "all of us, and especially you women, must have personal experience of all the nonsense of life, in order to get back to life itself; the evidence of other people is no good. At that time you had not got near the end of that charming nonsense which I admired in you. So I let you go through it alone, feeling that I had no right to put pressure on you, though my own time for that sort of thing was long past."

"If you loved me," I said, "how could you stand beside me and suffer me to go through it?"

"Because it was impossible for you to take my word for it, though you would have tried to. Personal experience was necessary, and now you have had it."

"There was much calculation in all that," I said, "but little love."

And again we were silent.

"What you said just now is severe, but it is true," he began, rising suddenly and beginning to walk about the veranda. "Yes, it is true. I was to blame," he added, stopping opposite me; "I ought either to have kept myself from loving you at all, or to have loved you in a simpler way."

"Let us forget it all," I said timidly.

"No," he said; "the past can never come back, never;" and his voice softened as he spoke.

"It is restored already," I said, laying a hand on his shoulder.

He took my hand away and pressed it.

"I was wrong when I said that I did not regret the past. I do regret it; I weep for that past love which can never return. Who is to blame, I do not know. Love remains, but not the old love; its place remains, but it all wasted away and has lost all strength and substance; recollections are still left, and gratitude; but . . ."

"Do not say that!" I broke in. "Let all be as it was before! Surely that is possible?" I asked, looking into his eyes; but their gaze was clear and calm, and did not look deeply into mine.

Even while I spoke, I knew that my wishes and my petition were impossible. He smiled calmly and gently; and I thought it the smile of an old man.

"How young you are still!" he said, "and I am so old. What you seek in me is no longer there. Why deceive ourselves?" he added, still smiling.

I stood silent opposite to him, and my heart grew calmer.

"Don't let us try to repeat life," he went on. "Don't let us make pretences to ourselves. Let us be thankful that there is an end of the old emotions and excitements. The excitement of searching is over for us; our quest is done, and happiness enough has fallen to our lot. Now we must stand aside and make room — for him, if you like," he said, pointing to the nurse who was carrying Vanya out and had stopped at the veranda door. "that's the truth, my dear one," he said, drawing down my head and kissing it, not a lover any longer but an old friend.

The fragrant freshness of the night rose ever stronger and sweeter from the garden; the sounds and the silence grew more solemn; star after star began to twinkle overhead. I looked at him, and suddenly my heart grew light; it seemed that the cause of my suffering had been removed like an aching nerve. Suddenly I realized clearly and calmly that the past feeling, like the past time itself, was gone beyond recall, and that it would be not only impossible but painful and uncomfortable to bring it back. And after all, was that time so good which seemed to me so happy? and it was all so long, long ago!

"Time for tea!" he said, and we went together to the parlour. At the door we met the nurse with the baby. I took him in my arms, covered his bare little red legs, pressed him to me, and kissed him with the lightest touch of my lips. Half asleep, he moved the parted fingers of one creased little hand and opened dim little eyes, as if he was looking for something or recalling something. all at once his eyes rested on me, a spark of consciousness shone in them, the little pouting lips, parted before, now met and opened in a smile. "Mine, mine, mine!" I thought, pressing him to my breast with such an impulse of joy in every limb that I found it hard to restrain myself from hurting him. I fell to kissing the cold little feet, his stomach and hand and head with its thin covering of down. My husband came up to me, and I quickly covered the child's face and uncovered it again.

"Ivan Sergeich!" said my husband, tickling him under the chin. But I made haste to cover Ivan Sergeich up again. None but I had any business to look long at him. I glanced at my husband. His eyes smiled as he looked at me; and Ii looked into them with an ease and happiness which I had not felt for a long time.

That day ended the romance of our marriage; the old feeling became a precious irrecoverable remembrance; but a new feeling of love for my children and the father of my children laid the foundation of a new life and a quite different happiness; and that life and happiness have lasted to the present time.